TODD

IAN GILBRAITH

ISBN-13: 979-8-9923962-3-2

Printed in the United States of America

Howl

Her children were gone.

Behind the darkest shroud of the deepest woods, between the shadowed husks of frozen trees, Wolfmother's den lay bare. Ripped apart from the inside out, trespassers had violated this sunken hut she called her home—little more than a cave with a front door that had been blown off its hinges by human wickedness. The druid paced back and forth over her threshold, as if she dared not venture too deep into her own home, now that these violators had tainted it with their rubber boots and metal tools. The busted hinges of the broken door stuck with frozen blood; Wolfmother sniffed at it tentatively. Not hers. Not her kin. Her children had fought back—good. They were growing quickly, raised well by their mother. She prayed they were prepared for their journey now, that they may yet fight back and escape. Failing that, she had only one choice:

She must call for Todd.

The name carried with it the ages of the forest itself, the lone sentinel that bridged worlds. Todd kept the humans out and the fey in. When the snows thawed in the spring and the humans drifted closer to the dark veil of this shadowed land, Todd sent them back to their fireplaces with scarred limbs and lessons learned. When creatures of the night crept towards the edges of the forest at first snowfall, Todd would be there to give the imps a thrashing and remind them of the terms of their confinement. Only the druids could come and go as they pleased, and rarely did they go.

Wolfmother had lived her human life, worn it to the bone; she'd not return as long as her cubs lived under her care.

The druid winced as she felt along her side; a redcap spear, little more than a flexible stick, a javelin fashioned from sappy wood and primitive craftsmanship. The foul primates that skirted the river's edge had crossed it several nights past, leaving the detritus of their latest kill in Wolfmother's territory. She'd ventured out to beat the creatures back across the river, and had narrowly avoided becoming their next meal—upwards of a dozen of them, an unusual counting, given their propensity for smaller family units. This tribe had become desperate and hungry in this deeper, colder winter, and weren't afraid of larger prey. Dangerous. As a consequence, Wolfmother felt their spears, and would need the help of the tengu medicines to remove the weapon without bleeding out.

She was in no shape to go running out into the snow after the Violators, after her cubs.

Spitting a wad of saliva to rid her nostrils of the smell of human blood, Wolfmother stepped back into the snow, her shoulders rolling back as the fur sprouted and her neck broadened. The wind blew the knotted human hair across her face as her features shifted, giving quiet death to the portrait of her former life as the wolf's snout sprouted forth to take its place. A human's cry would not carry on this icy wind. Todd would only answer the call of a fellow beast.

Wolfmother took a knee as her torso followed the way of her lupine flesh, her head already wolfen before the changes had reached her belly—raising her muzzle skyward, she howled out her pain and need, her voice carried by the wind above the gnarled branches of the canopy above. The moonless night howled its response, acknowledging her call, the wind making the stiff trees crack and groan. The message was away, and the winter storm would do the rest, a wolf's howl echoing all about the shadowed valley.

*

The call reached Todd's ears, arriving with the midnight flurries of snow, miles away from its origin. In that distant howl, Todd heard all that was needed: failure, desperation, and loss. Wolfmother had little to lose, save for her family. Had she any other reason to call for aid, Todd may not have answered—as it was, this particularly cold night found Todd in a charitable mood, swayed by the cold sting of memories that threatened to settle in for the night. Kidnapping was the perfect distraction from the solitude, and Todd shook off the snow as she rose from her slumber.

Overhead, a nightbird croaked in surprise, stirred by the shifting of the great beast below. Weeks had gone by without so much as a twitch from Todd, and when she rose now, it was with purpose. Speed was needed now, if indeed Wolfmother's children were gone—the takers would be on their way out of these shadowed woods before the storm became too fierce. Todd would, of course, never let them get that far—a little blizzard never slowed her before.

The nightbird watched with tilted head as the dark underbrush became a flurry of activity, the dark shape of the forest guardian within waking from her hibernation. The dull thud of heavy limbs against packed snow, the crunch of withered branches beneath expansive bulk—Todd was stamping her feet to shake off the ice, to work up her heartrate, raise her body temperature. Tonight, the hunt was afoot, and the old beast needed to stay warm: the storm meant to ensnare her, slow her wits.

Todd knew the answer to the storm—if children were missing, the only proper response was rage.

The underbrush exploded outwards around the massive shadow, and the great beast was off, sending the nightbird flapping upwards into the night in a panic. The call had come from the valley below, and Todd's mountain rose high above it. Gravity would lend her speed for the time being. The forest guardian was a cannonball through the dead trees, sending sonic blasts of icicles and shards of wood all about as she hurtled down the slopes, bound for the south valley. Todd's sheer momentum would flatten the mountain itself if it had stood in her way; wisely, the mountain decided to step aside tonight.

The warden of the woods was awake, and not even the storm was prepared.

*

The first leg of her journey was a short one indeed. The mountain slope began to peter off, and Todd's limbs worked harder now to carry her forward, her speed borne now of her own heart's engine. The trees began to thin, and the snow thicken: Wolfmother's den was getting close, and Todd could hear the screams.

The clearing ahead, illuminated only by Todd's gift of nocturnal sight, the white of the snow acting as canvas upon which the black ink of the forest had been painted—and when the trees parted, the ink spilled, painting a stark picture indeed. Wolfmother was assailed on all sides by a pack of redcaps, the druid having fully shifted into her animal form. Thin, reed-like spears jutted from her back and sides; the wolf whirled about in strokes of black and white and red, her grey fur steaming with blood. Her jaws snapped uselessly at air, the redcaps dancing just out of reach of her fangs; the wolf's strength was failing.

There was nothing for it now—Wolfmother stumbled backwards, towards her den, and with the redcaps advancing on her, spears raised, her very human voice wailed out a single word above the rising dirge of the snowstorm:

"TO-O-O-DD!"

The answer came in an instant. The treeline exploded around the arrival of the summoned beast, a tidal wave of snow crashing down on the heads of the redcaps, sending the furred apes scampering in fear. They turned now, hopping mad, chittering at one another as all their attention was pulled away from Wolfmother and placed now on this new arrival: the enormous shadow sent by the storm. Even in their stupid little brains, they knew they were not the intended target for this beast's ire.

But they were definitely in her way.

Todd rose up on her hind legs, and with the voice of the ancient forest itself escaping her lungs, the giant werebear roared down at the pitiful homunculi below—loud enough to frighten away the storm itself, if only for a moment. The hateful destroyer's eyes burned with all the fury of a grizzly whose winter slumber had been disturbed; her snout wrapped with the ribbons of saliva that dripped off her gleaming fangs.

The doomed little monkeys tried in vain to hide behind one another—the redcaps, so-called because of the crimson wattles that stood straight up from the bridge of their short snouts, now found their wattles flagging weakly, shrinking much like their other unmentionables at the sight of Todd. In numbers like these, they may stand a chance at taking down a lone wolf; even if they numbered in the thousands, they knew there was no hope against an old werebear.

But these redcaps were particularly hungry, and particularly stupid, emboldened by their near kill tonight. They screeched back at Todd, echoing the bear's roar without even a teenth of her rage, giving this intruder their answer: they were not surrendering their chance at fresh meat tonight.

Good news for Todd. She would need the protein for the rest of her journey.

The enraged bear came down on the redcaps with all the ceremony of a falling boulder, scattering their furry little bodies in the shockwave. Before they had a chance to scramble back to their feet, she was in their midst, snapping up the little imps in her wet maw. They screamed and pounded at her head with tiny fists, going limp as she bit down, crushing their bodies in her viselike jaws. Tossing one aside, she moved onto the next— long forelimbs scooped them up before they could escape, obsidian claws raking their bodies and heads, tossing them like paper dolls. The white snow quickly turned spotty red, and in seconds, their numbers dwindled to almost nothing.

Swallowing down a severed leg, Todd whipped about, her great bulk wobbling—her eyes fixed on the remaining three redcaps, and once more she roared out her challenge, face and lips stained with their fallen comrades.

The message finally getting through to them, the primates snatched up their fallen spears in shaky hands, bolting for the trees— their previous kill by the river's edge would have to satisfy what was left of their mighty tribe now.

On all fours now, Todd huffed, clearing her nostrils of splattered redcap. She lumbered forward, towards Wolfmother—she had no time for conversation, and Wolfmother knew it. The wounded wolf limped aside, looking to the doorframe, and Todd stepped in close to investigate. Her nose trailed up and down the frozen splashes of blood, drinking in the scent of her chosen quarry. It was faint, but it was enough—the blizzard hadn't arrived in time to fully conceal the trail that led into the trees, away from the river and the mountain alike.

Todd was southbound once more. She brushed past Wolfmother dismissively—the werebear was no healer, and she offered no promises or words of comfort. It wasn't her job to console grieving mothers. It was her job to protect the forest and its children. The wolf understood, shrinking back into her den to await the arrival of a woodland spirit—her howl would have alerted any nearby, just as it had Todd.

The hunt was on, and with a deep breath to focus the scent of the trail in her mind, Todd set off again into the trees. The bear knew every inch of these shadowlands, this forest having been her home for centuries.

She'd taste the flesh of these child thieves before the sun rose.

Splinter

If these woods ever had a name, it was long since lost to time, just as its existence was forgotten by outside civilization. The Shadowlands existed in a vacuum, the forest behind the world, accessible only by slipping through the gap in the curtains of reality. Only those especially skilled or those touched by the Other Side knew how to find such a gap. That, or they would need to have their route drawn for them by someone who knew the nature of such spacial mysticism. Todd had every reason to suspect the latter was the case, as anyone who knew the Shadowlands existed at all would know well enough to leave its inhabitants unmolested. There were always consequences to interfering with fey matter; dip one uninvited toe into the waters of the spirit realms, you risked losing a leg.

It made for the perfect refuge for Todd. A refuge from the memories she'd left behind at the edge of these woods, many years ago.

Todd had pulled every string she had with God to remain undisturbed in her later years, and it seemed God had other plans for her—even now, as she sprinted through the night, away from even the most remote human settlement, she felt the memories creeping back. They tickled at her mind like spiders tapping a web, and with nothing but the rushing wind and repeating thud of her own footfalls to keep her thoughts occupied, the spiders moved in to spin their gossamer treachery. The werebear was a druid, just as Wolfmother was—and much like Wolfmother, Todd had left the human world behind, seeking refuge in this hidden forest. But even spending her years transformed into a bear, speaking not a word to anyone, she was unable to tear herself from the silence that deafened her with these accursed memories.

The spiders would feast on her brain tonight, just as she would feast on the abductors who had taken Wolfmother's cubs. Todd had no choice but to endure their venom as it coursed through her, filling her mind's eye once more with their spiteful images.

*

"You don't think it's a little too flimsy?"

"I think if you keep trying to poke holes in everything, it will be."

They'd spend the afternoon assembling the bassinet, and the evening light was bathing the baby's bedroom in its yellow glow. Todd wrapped her arms around Timber's neck, her slender frame hanging off of his built muscles as easily as a scarf. "I just don't want you to get lazy and start rocking it with your foot, then you end up kicking the poor kid out the window."

Timber laughed, cupping a hand around his wife's elbow. "He's gotta leave home someday, might as well give him an early start. Prepare him for the hardships of the real world, y'know?"

"Yeah, good point." Todd released her husband from the chokehold, focusing her attention on her thumb. "Ow. Got a splinter."

"Here, lemme suck it out."

Todd slapped at Timber's nose playfully to repel him. "Don't. Gonna get it infected. Speaking of early starts, when's the last time you brushed your teeth? Your breath smells like booze."

The baby was crying from the other room—Timber didn't answer his wife, opting to answer their child instead as he turned away from her. "Hang on, kid's upset. I got him this time. Don't you have work soon?"

"Yeah, just as soon as I get this splinter out." Todd watched her husband disappear down the hall, turning once more to her thumb. It was a stubborn one—she could see the little green flecks of it coming away beneath her nail as she tried scraping it out. "Hey babe, you know where the medical tape is?" She called out down the hall.

No answer. Even the baby was quiet now. Todd poked her head out into the dark hallway. "Tim?" She called out.

Still, there was only silence. She walked forward, stepping out of the baby's room, heading for the den—

*

Todd stumbled, snarling out in pain. A sharp hunk of tree branch had embedded itself beneath the claws of her forepaw, slowing her pace to almost nothing. With a vengeance she ripped it free between her teeth, spitting the oversized splinter away. The wound it left behind was small, but it bled freely—she pressed the whole paw into the snow forcefully, letting the cold attend to it.

She hadn't intended for her mind to wander to that specific moment in time, nor did she relish the prospect of inhabiting that memory any longer than she already had. Todd tested her weight on the injured limb, mentally willing herself past that proverbial bear trap. Nothing would slow her pace tonight, least of all something as intangible as her own memories.

Todd pointed her nose forward, and once again she was off at a steady pace, giving herself time to numb the wound in the snow before hitting her full stride again. It was a momentary distraction, but unfortunately the spiders were not done with her yet. Their threads closed in on her once more, wrapping her vision in white cloth—

*

Todd threw down her cards on the tablecloth, leaning back in her creaky chair to take another drag of her cigarillo, the blue smoke rising to the low ceiling of the dimly lit cabin. "I'm tapped," she declared, waving the smoke away, along with her bad luck. "Last hand for me tonight, I gotta be up early."

"Taking care of the kid tomorrow?" Leah asked, the younger woman adding another scale to the pool.

"Nah, Timber's got him again—I promised I'd help Ma out at the outpost, she's winding down for the season." Todd coughed into her fist, soothing her throat with another pull on the cig. "Though I'd be lying if I said I'm looking forward to it."

"Why do you still go up there?" The woman over Todd's shoulder was attending to a sizzling pan, cooking up a decidedly unhealthy dinner for the girls tonight. Channi gave the pan a toss without even looking, turning to Todd with a frown. "Isn't it about time you called it quits with the old gal?"

"I agree, believe me," Todd answered, expelling the smoke from between her pursed lips. "I don't have anything in common with her. Just...if I don't take care of her, there's no one else to step in for me. Like it or not I'm stuck."

"It's not your job to take care of everyone," Henrietta argued as Todd stood up from the table. "You keep running yourself ragged like this, there isn't gonna be enough of you left for us to bleed dry at these card games."

Todd waggled her eyebrows in response, mouth puckered around her cig as she looped her arms into the sleeves of her heavy coat.

"Having a kid's gotta be plenty of work on its own, anyway," Channi continued, scraping the contents of the pan onto a few dishes. "Can't be expected to be in two places and caring for two families at once. Sure you don't want some of this before you go?"

"Nah I'm good. I just—" Todd paused as she sucked on the cig, pulling it from her lips and blowing the smoke out thoughtfully. "It's Tim. He keeps insisting I spend more and more time up there with Ma, but. I just get this feeling anytime I leave him alone with the kid..."

"What kind of feeling?"

Todd didn't answer, lost in her own thoughts. She shrugged, tamping the cig out in the dish next to the door as she pulled the coat in tight. "Thanks for the drinks, I'll catch you all next week. I'll see about bringing down some of Ma's smoked venison when I come back 'round."

The girls 'ooh'ed in response to this as Todd shoved open the door, the blue smoke swirling around her as she stepped out into the snow—

*

The fire had been burning up until only very recently, left unattended by the hunters when they'd located their prize. Todd circled the smoldering logs, sniffing at the wind, her nostrils stinging from the harsh smoke. Letting the storm snuff it out meant they'd been in a hurry. Which meant they didn't care much for cleaning up their tracks behind him. Which meant they were sloppy. Sloppy was good, it meant less time snuffling about in the dark for Todd.

There was a flipside to this luck, though, even if she didn't want to admit it. Less time occupying her thoughts with where to go and how to proceed meant more time letting her mind wander. More time reminiscing on these intrusive memories.

Why tonight, of all nights? Why these memories?

She didn't know or care, but it pissed her off to no end. The bear swiped at the dying embers of the campfire, snuffing it out beneath a wash of dirt and snow. There was a baby crying in her ears, and she could hear it even over the sound of the wind—it was unlikely that it was coming from anywhere out in those woods. Todd tried to stifle the noise by continuing to nose about the camp, digging up anything she could find beneath the scattered trash left behind by the hunters. Paper wrappings, metal clips, some wood shavings from something one of them had been carving—

There, more blood. Todd set upon it, parsing the smells carefully: there was more than one source time. One she recognized as the same human who had bled on Wolfmother's stoop. The other was decidedly not human, most likely that of a young wolf. One of the cubs had fought back and drawn blood. The hunter had retaliated in punishment. Todd envisioned the scene in her mind, the older sister standing up to the hunter, protecting her younger brother. She'd taken a beating in return. Good girl— don't let 'em off easy. Give them a reason to waste time on you, waste resources keeping you in check. The more they delayed, the faster Todd could close the gap. It had been almost a full day now since they'd passed through here, and despite her confidence in herself, Todd knew she'd need all the help she could get if the storm got any worse, as it likely would.

Or if these memories kept getting in the way.

Todd shook her head, attempting to dislodge the clinging cobwebs within. She knew it wouldn't be so easy, however.

Splinter

However long this chase would last, she knew she was in for a long night.

Tight

Above the lakehouse, the early morning fog was giving way to the late morning rainclouds rolling in, the gray curtain sweeping over the lake far from shore—though it would likely be coming down on their heads within the hour. Todd was in the process of unloading the rover, Timber having taken the kids inside to say hello to their grandmother; Jeanie was too young to do much of anything but fuss in Timber's arms, but Judd had taken off like a bolt of lightning the second his feet had touched wet gravel. Making the drive up to the caldera was always tedious, even with their rover being so well-equipped for the terrain—it was almost a vertical incline once they cleared the snowcaps, and the last leg of the trip was always the slowest. Todd didn't blame her son for wanting to stretch his legs.

She let the heaviest suitcase fall at her feet, knowing there was nothing fragile inside—though that didn't stop her mother from complaining, the older druid stepping out of the lakehouse just in time to see Todd drop the bag, Jeanie cradled in her arms.

"Don't just throw shit around, girl," Niju barked, making Jeanie giggle as she dressed down the infant's mother. "I know I damn sure raised you better than that."

"Ma, please, language," Todd complained, already feeling the aches setting in about her neck and shoulders. "She's right at the age where she's gonna start repeating everything you say."

"Oh, perfect, then she'll be able to join the chorus in thanking me for what a bang-up fuckin' job I did teaching you to take better care of your belongings." Niju brushed aside her bangs, the beads woven into her long hair clicking together. "I set a bath for Timber. Dirty bastard. You mind your training your husband in matters of basic hygiene before you next darken my stoop?"

"Cut him a break, he's stressed from losing that big contract is all," Todd argued, sighing as she wiped a forearm across her face. "You mind not treating my husband like a child? It'd go a long way in not making these trips of ours such a drag on you, as you say."

"Keep him in line, I won't have to." Niju sniffed airily, turning her nose up. "Judd's run out to the boathouse. Gonna be taking him out fishing later on, weather should drum up the deep swimmers."

"Ma, are you serious? He just got over a cold. And why are you letting him play around in the boathouse by himself, he's gonna get himself hurt." Todd abandoned the task at hand, making a beeline across the gravel yard towards the boathouse. "For being so concerned about my family unit, you sure do seem to enjoy setting them up for failure."

"Your problem is you're too soft on 'em," Niju retorted, not bothering to follow Todd to the boathouse as she raised her voice after her daughter. "You forget where you came from, girl? They're meant for bigger things than idling away at that abattoir you call a 'school'."

"Not if I can help it," Todd whispered to herself as she opened the boathouse door, rubbing at her neck tenderly. These trips to visit Ma never failed to put the stress on her shoulders.

The moment the doors swung open, she heard splashing and a small, strangled voice sobbing.

"Judd?" Todd's head whipped about—the boy was nowhere to be seen, Niju's schooner the only source of movement besides herself in the small space.

"Down here! Help me!"

The voice was coming from below the dock the schooner was moored to. Todd rushed forward, crouching down to look over the edge.

Her son had fallen in between the boat and the embankment, one leg hooked over the mooring line, his other dangling low enough to kick against the surface of the water. Red-faced and teary-eyed, he wriggled helplessly, keeping himself upright with both arms sandwiched between himself and the dock. "Help, mommy, please!" He cried again, fat tears rolling down his cheeks.

"Godammit," Todd hissed, quickly lowering herself off the edge of the dock. She held onto the concrete embankment above with both hands, hooking her boots along the lower edge, just above the water's surface. She shimmied along, inching closer to where Judd had fallen. "Hang on, baby, I'm coming, just hold tight."

"I'm slipping!" Judd wailed, his knuckles white and his fingertips purple. If Todd wasn't quick, he could fall and drown—or even be crushed between the boat and the dock, considering the way the weather was making the water kick up, making the schooner rock dangerously.

"Just hold tight, I'm almost there!" Todd held her breath, squeezing herself in closer to the concrete, deliberately wedging herself into the tight space as she reached out—

*

The sheer rock wall was too steep and icy to climb over, too wide-spanning to make the hike around without losing several hours. As Todd looked into the narrow crevice that passed between where the rock face had split, she knew the only way through was exactly that—through. And there was no way she was fitting into that gap in her current form.

It had been decades since she'd last shifted, and a larger part of her had always assumed she'd never do it again. The werebear took a big, shuddering breath, recalling that inner part of herself that anchored her forms, that knot of magic that had been transposed upon her soul at birth. She dug her claws into the snow, remembering the feeling of cold against fleshy fingertips, the way frost melted against pink palms—

The great paws of a grizzly bear melted away into filthy knuckles, the arms slimming down in seconds, the excess matter whisked away to some NetherRealm beyond the physical. The bear rocked back on her hips, her weight dissipating, thick and blubbery pelt being replaced with layers of hemp cloth and assorted animal furs. Eventually, the painless transition completed, and Todd opened her human eyes for the first time in years. The cold wind bit at her exposed cheeks, and she shivered—she'd forgotten how much of a shock the difference in her bodies' temperatures were. Reaching down, Todd pulled up her scarf like a mask to shield her face, stepping forward towards the gap in the rock face. The sooner she could get through to the other side and return to bear form, the better.

The craggy stone was razor ice to the touch. Clenching her fists momentarily to stimulate blood-flow, Todd squeezed herself into the gap, sucking in her chest to keep her breasts from scraping the frozen rock wall. She shimmied along sideways, inch by inch, determined not to let this momentary lapse in her pace keep her at bay—if those assholes had passed through here without a problem, then she sure as shit wouldn't let a few moments of cold hold her back.

Still, she couldn't help but shiver, finding the impulse nigh uncontrollable as her body temperature declined rapidly. Todd distracted herself by digging her fingertips against the rock, as if she still had claws—the pain refocused her attention just enough to keep her feet moving quickly, and soon she saw the daylight filtering in through the other side of the gap. She looked up, high above her head. The wind whistled between the rock walls, an eerie, longing sound. Snowflakes fell from high above, melting against her eyelashes as she blinked them away.

The gap grew tighter and tighter, threatening to pull the animal furs off her shoulders—grunting, Todd pushed on, reaching out with a hand. Soon enough, she couldn't feel stone anymore, only open air—

And then she was on the other side, stumbling free of the narrow gap, her snowshoes crunching on wet gravel. Todd panted, sucking in a deep breath, finding the air strangely warm. She looked about at the clearing she stood in now: it seemed untouched by snow, and indeed, steam began to rise off the patches of her flesh not covered by fur or cloth. She was standing at the edge of a large pond, warmth rising off the surface of the water, the sound of insects buzzing all about.

Todd shrugged off the animal pelts, suddenly on edge. This was not a natural occurrence—a glade like this, in the middle of the shadowed forest, during a blizzard? That could only mean—

"Siwmae—d'you know how close you came to being mulched into a bloody paste just then? Gave me a right fright, ya did."

Todd sucked on her teeth, shaking her head. She knew what she was in for before even raising her head to look at the stranger addressing her: a piebald raven, his white and black feathers standing out brightly against the lush green backdrop of the moist tree canopy. The bird appraised Todd with the typical mischievous air of a tengu spirit, leaning towards her with one limb raised off his branch.

"I'm not interested today," Todd answered back, trying in vain to keep the annoyed tone out of her voice. "I've a long ways to go and not enough time to get there."

"That's unfortunate," the raven replied, preening himself under the wing dismissively. "Afraid I don't get 'nuff visitors to pass up a chance to make friends, and the gormless blokes who passed through just this morn proved themselves proper dullards, they did."

"Oh yeah?" Todd shifted tactics, suddenly curious. "Tell me about them. How many were there? Did they look like hunters?"

"Naughty naughty. You'll not change the subject on me, lass; I cannae abide the sneaky type—present company notwithstanding," the raven said with a demonstrative wave of the wing towards himself. "You'll play my game, or you'll nae leave this pretty little glade. As it so happens, I've a need for a new bearskin rug."

The green loam at Todd's feet began to wriggle—she took a half-step backwards, coolly avoiding the patch of nightcrawlers that had burrowed their way to the surface, their blood-red bodies squirming in a disgusting puddle. "You can sense I'm a druid, then," Todd said, remaining calm. "So, you wouldn't be surprised to hear I don't have anything to offer as payment, and I've lived my whole life in these woods—I know just as much as you do about the outside world, which makes me terrible at riddles."

"Aye! Lies upon lies. Very naughty indeed." The raven hopped closer, the branch freezing over behind him in an instant before it thawed once more, dripping with melted frost—the illusion had been momentarily disturbed, restored once the raven found himself another perch. He drew himself up, puffing out his white chest feathers. "D'ya kiss your mae with that lying mouth, lass?"

Todd glared back silently, her hackles rising. The raven nodded, satisfied. "Mm, a sore subject, I see. Splendid. Family, eh? Cannae live with 'em, cannae be apart from 'em before a charming little imp has a chance to pick at the old scabs they left you with. No matter—I'll have my fun, you'll be on your way. Behave, and all it'll cost ye is a small piece of your soul."

"You'll find I taste funny," Todd snarked, walking around the edge of the steaming pond, drawing closer to the raven. It was impossible to see past the illusion to tell what was really there, but she had a feeling it wasn't a pool of warm water.

"And you'll find I've a taste for rot and rank, dearie," the raven crooned. "Now, manners! I go by many names—"

"—Which are too innumerable to list, so instead you'll give me one you just made up—"

"—Which are too—ah!" The raven croaked happily. "Played before, have ye? Excellent! Then I'll spare ye the tutorial. In the meanst-times, call me 'Cornell', if it pleases ye."

"Cornell it is, then." Todd sat herself upon a mossy rock, crossing her arms impatiently. "I'll have your riddle. Shoot."

"Straight to the point, eh? Tsk, typical." Cornwall swayed to and fro on his branch as he spoke, giving cadence to the riddle as he recited:

It is in the rock, yet nae in the stone;

It is in the marrow, yet nae in the bone;

It is in the bolster, yet nae in the bed;

It is nae in the living—nae, still, in the dead."

Todd thought for a moment, then scoffed. She'd heard this one before. "Easy. The letter 'R'—can I go now?"

She stood to leave, but found the illusion persisted, and was buffeted back by a gust of wind from the raven's wings.

"Nae, nae!" Cornell cackled. "A daft schoolchild couldae guessed that'un. Nae, 'fraid that was a warmup, sweetheart. Settle in—the real thing is a doozy."

"You're wasting my time," Todd growled, resisting the urge to shift then and there—she'd seen what happened firsthand when someone tried to use their magics on a tengu. "Ask your question, or get out of my way."

There was a horrific screech of agony, the sound filling the glade and sending a few frogs diving from their lilypads. Partway up the length of the tree Cornell was using as his perch, a dark hollow began to stir—then, from within the gaping orifice, a limb extended. A human arm, peeled of flesh, the red muscle fibers beneath exposed to the elements—it shuddered as it reached towards Todd, dripping viscera. Then, following close behind, the head of

Cornell's victim emerged—eyeless sockets gazed at Todd, pleading for salvation from this torment, another strangled scream escaping the skinned man's pulsating throat.

"Dullards, as I said." Cornell tossed his beak back, barely paying the living corpse any mind. "They were in a right hurry, as well. Me? I like to slow things way, way down."

He raised a wing, and thorny branches lashed out to wrap around the man's forehead, digging into his scalped flesh. The tree yanked the skinned man back, disappearing him into the darkness once more. The screaming disappeared with him. Todd knew it could be years before the man ever knew death.

Sighing, the druid took her seat once more. She didn't cross her arms this time.

Tight

"Alright, Cornell. Let's hear it."

Riddles

"Tim?"

The house was dark; nobody answered. Todd closed the back door behind her as she entered, taking care not to shut the latch too loudly, in case she missed hearing a response. There was none.

"Hey, Tim? Kids?" She slipped out of her leather boots, padding softly down the dark hallway, towards the den. She passed the kids' room as she went—she didn't need to look inside to know it was empty, the door left ajar. The only visible light was at the end of the hall, coming from within the den—Todd could hear the quiet clink of ice in a glass.

Timber was home after all, ignoring her. Todd stood in the wide doorway, looking at

Timber, sitting in his chair—his eyes were as dark as the rest of the house as he set down his drink, and Todd was becoming more and more nervous by the second.

"Tim? Where are the kids?"

"You were supposed to have been back days ago." Timber stood from his seat, trying to keep steady on his feet—he'd been hitting the bottle hard. "I don't expect you to be honest with me all the time, but *some* of the time would be nice."

Todd stood her ground as Timber approached. "Tim, where are my kids?"

He stopped short of her, looming over her—he tittered, shaking his head. "You know, I used to find you so...intimidating. You were like a giant next to me. God knows how I ever let myself be fooled like that." He sniffed, turning his back on Todd to retrieve his drink. "I left the kids at your mom's place. They don't need to be around you right now."

"And what do they need, Tim?" Todd stepped into the den, her skin prickly—she always felt this way when she lost her patience, but rarely did she feel this way around family. "Why don't you help me out here, because I don't have a clue what you're talking about."

Tim took a long pull on his glass, shrugging in the process—the motion made him stumble somewhat. He spread his arms pleadingly, letting loose a wet laugh. "A mother? Maybe? Someone here to raise them, support them? Someone who gives a shit about them?"

"You're drunk. That's over the line, Tim—I'd never say something like that about you." Todd crossed the room, brushing past Tim roughly to cap off the bottle sitting on the table. Tim stared down at her, unbalanced, eyes bleary with fat tears that had yet to fall.

"I thought you cared about me, too. About us. I don't know what I did to make you hate me so much, Todd—haven't I always been here for you when you came home? Haven't I always been here to take care of you when you were hurt? You know, you keep heading out on these little adventures of yours, living this double life—I'm gonna get to thinking here soon that you don't want to be here anymore. With us. You know what that's like? What that does to me? How that makes me feel? How it makes the kids feel?"

"I don't have time for this. Are you coming with me to pick up the kids or not? And how many times have I told you to keep your fucking shoes outside when you come home?"

Todd picked up Timber's muddy boots, leaving grimy prints behind in the carpet. Tim grabbed at her arm. "Hey—slow down for a second, babe. Just—can you talk to me? Just talk to me for a second?"

His grip wasn't tight enough to hurt, but Todd nevertheless felt the back of her neck tingle. She narrowed her eyes. "Let go of my arm."

Timber leaned in close, speaking softly. "I'm your husband. You love me. You know I'd never hurt—*could* never hurt you. You know that, right?"

"I don't care. Let go."

Tim released his grip, holding his hands up in surrender. "Okay. I'm sorry. I apologize. You know it's just—I'm trying to talk to you here, and you're trying to run off, like always. You're always ignoring me, how I feel—"

"Spare me the victim act, Tim, I know how you feel about me when you're drunk." Todd tossed the muddy boots into the hall, sending flakes of dried mud scattering all across the wood floors. "You know, my 'double life', as you say, is exactly what you wanted. You knew what you were getting into when we got married—don't try to pin all this on me now that you're out of work and can't find a use for yourself. Make some friends, get a hobby. I've changed enough for you to make this life work—don't ask me to change anymore."

Timber stared at her incredulously. "I never asked for that. I never asked you to change. I loved you the way you were, day one." He stepped forward, gently cupping her shoulders under his calloused palms. "All of you, everything about you. Even the angry side. I loved that you could make me feel safe as easy as make me feel scared. I loved that you adopted this whole mountaintop just to give us a community to be part of. D'you know how many guys in the village can say their wife is a shapeshifting freedom fighter? How cool that makes me sound when I talk about you at the bar?"

"I'm not gonna tell you again. Take your hands off me."

Tim was stunned. "Take my hands— Todd! It's me. Remember me? Where are you right now? Where have you gone? Come back to me, please. I miss you. The kids miss—"

It wasn't a scrawny woman that spoke next. Timber was tossed backwards, something in his arm cracking wetly as he slammed into the wall. He yelped out, clutching at his elbow, shrinking in fear as he looked up at the grizzly bear filling the den now. Todd had shifted in an instant, her claws flexing—she'd never threatened him like this before.

They both knew she'd fucked up. The snarling bear quieted, withdrawing into herself, and moments later Todd was standing in the doorway once more. She cautiously approached, the slender woman holding her hands out in front of her, eyes wide and panicked.

"Shh, I'm sorry, it's okay," Todd said, her voice low and husky. She paused when Timber recoiled, kneeling in front of him. Something had snapped in her, and she didn't know what—and for the first time in her life, she felt fear. In the scuffle, something had fallen from the shelf above Timber's head, landing on the floor beside him—Todd scooped it up in shaky hands. It was a wooden carving of a bear, something Judd had made for her one lazy afternoon, barely lighter than a pinecone. She held it close to her chest.

"It's okay, I'm sorry," Todd repeated. She wrapped her arms around her husband, taking care not to touch his broken arm. "I don't know what's wrong with me. Please, I'm sorry—"

*

Riddles

"*What tears into flesh without tooth or claw.*

Invisible wounds that ceaselessly weep;

What icy season refuses to thaw,

The storm that denies the dreamer his sleep?

Take all you can carry, and walk with the dead,

And there'll be naught left of you to bury;

Keep none at all, less weight on your head,

And become the weight the living must carry."

Todd shook her head. "And if I don't know the answer?"

Cornell danced on his branch happily. "Then I get paid! What trinkets have ye? A shiny bauble to buy your way out of my riddle, me hopes!"

Todd reached beneath the furs draped over her shoulders, into her vest. Concealed within, she gripped the small, hard object, pulling it out to appraise it quietly. The wooden bear carving, weathered and chipped, the paint faded from years of neglect. It was the only piece of her former life she still carried with her in these woods. She'd almost forgot she still had it.

"If I decide against that, too?"

Cornell stopped dancing. The air chilled about Todd as he replied.

"Then I get creative with ye. And I've been feeling rather fucking bored as of late."

Todd knew all-too well there would be consequences if she refused the raven's game.

Yet, despite this, she found herself unable—or unwilling—to revisit the riddle. She had very quickly forgotten it, suppressing the words behind a wall of her own stubbornness. The alternative was to give up the one thing she had to offer; looking at it now, Todd was unwilling to part with that, either. It seemed she was stuck here, unable to proceed.

That wasn't an option for her either. There were young lives at stake.

So, pocketing the bear carving once more, Todd stared up at Cornell defiantly.

"You said you like to take things slow, yeah?" She cocked her head. "Maybe I need some more time to think about your riddle. A lot more time. Hours, even."

Cornell shivered on his branch, winging away some stray flecks of snow that filtered into the warm glade from somewhere beyond. "Unwise, lass, unwise indeed—nae against the rules, but nae how you get on my good side, either. The punishment for denying me twice could cost ye an eternity."

Todd stood once more. She raised her voice, repeating her answer. "I need more time. Come find me, later tonight. Once I've done what needs to be done, I'll have figured out your riddle. That, or I'll have something more valuable to pay you with. In either case: would you kindly fuck off for now?"

The tengu radiated a dangerous haze of distrust. He crackled with invisible electricity, primeval forces backing him. His displeasure made the hairs on the back of Todd's neck stand up.

"I'll find ye, indeed I will, nae worries 'boot that." Cornell shimmered in Todd's vision, carefully undoing the illusion that shrouded him from the real world. "Though I'd pray to your gods you have your answer by then—else your gods will be prayin' for ye, instead."

And with that, he vanished—along with the mirage he'd created. Once more, Todd was standing in the cold, almost knee deep in the snow. She looked down, at her feet—as she suspected, there was no pond to speak of. Instead, a pit had been dug into the snow, carefully concealed by stray branches and dead bushes. Someone had fallen through, directly into the hidden trap, impaling themselves on the chiseled wooden spikes embedded within.

Todd kneeled beside the pit, reaching in carefully. The man was dressed like a hunter alright, though the garb itself was still peculiar—almost too professional-looking to be a private venture. Indeed, the man seemed to have a nametag of some kind. She yanked it free of his jacket, snapping the tiny karabiner fastening it in place. Todd wiped a hand across the nametag, cleaning it of snow and blood. Only his last name had been embossed on the tag, no other identifying characteristics. It read:

CORNELL

"Well, that's just lazy." Todd slipped the nametag into her vest. She looked to the dead tree across the pit, at the dark hollow partway up its length—it remained silent, empty. Home only to a ghost, now. The human named Cornell had not answered the tengu's riddle to his satisfaction, it seemed.

Flexing her neck and shoulders until they popped, Todd began to shift once more. Her human clothes dissipated in a puff of dark fog, the fur and bulk of the bear sprouting from her flesh, replacing everything about her that seemed fragile or weak—the bear didn't care about riddles or trinkets. Only the hunt. And she'd lost precious time, wasting it on these otherworldly games of make believe.

The bear charged forward, into the snow and trees once more, leaving behind the illusive glade. Cornell was a problem for her human self now. She'd have to deal with him in due time.

Candle

Years in these woods created a profile of scents in Todd's memory banks, the possible smells all limited to those naturally occurring elements—kudlik oil and arctic willows; the spicy Nor'western Poppy and cinnamon bark; waxy pine needles, aromatic spruce and other conifers. There was the rare lennox berry bush in the warmer months of spring, but besides that, it all blended together into the familiar— so when a foreign odor crept into the forest, Todd would sniff it out in no time at all. She'd been following the stiff scent of rubberized tools and human body odor for hours now, though it wasn't until something else hooked itself into her olfactories that she knew she was getting closer: a meaty, tangy scent, processed and seasoned. Manmade food of some kind, pulled from a private stash. The kind of snack someone would save for when supplies ran low and they needed a protein fix.

The trail ahead descended into a dense copse of trees, the canopy of skeletal branches becoming so thick and entangled that it remained dark and foreboding even on the brightest summer day. During a midnight blizzard, it was positively black. Lucky for Todd, eyesight wasn't much needed; a mile or so through the thicket, and she'd be on the other side, close to the edge of the forest. It was a straight shot now, so long as she followed her nose and kept on a linear path.

Todd kept her nose low, snuffling about to keep the scent of the meaty snack fresh in her mind, trudging along into the denser forest.

*

The bell rang above her head as she swung the creaky wooden door open, shuffling her coat to dust off some of the loose snow from her shoulders. "Joules, why's it so dark in here? Ever heard of electricity?"

The stout man at the counter shifted on his stool, leaning back to flip on the light switch—immediately, the general store was bathed in the yellow luminescence of cigar-smoked lightbulbs, their crystal fixtures likely older than anyone who visited this place.

"All 'pologies, lost track of time." Joules tamped out his stogie, fanning away the smoke with a nearby stack of telegram papers. "Though I'd be lyin' if I said I was expectin' anymore customers t'day—you, least of all."

Todd meandered through the cozy little store, dragging her gloved hands along the dusty shelves, only half-browsing what they had to offer. "That makes two of us. I fought myself for a good reason not to come out today, but I got one whiff of that appleroot-bison jerky of yours—couldn't resist it if I tried."

Joules scoffed, cracking a peppernut between his molars. "Bullshit. Ain't nobody like my jerky."

"Then why make it?"

Joules blinked, seeming confused by the silly question. "How else am I s'posed to sell the jerky if there ain't no one makin' it what for to be sold?"

Todd pointed back at Joules, nodding sheepishly. "Good point." She continued on, stopping at a rack of baskets, each filled with various booklets and ledgers. She pulled one out, appraising it with a wry smile. "Ah. Still carrying these old augury calendars, huh?"

"Keeps the housewives busy. Gives 'em cause to get creative with their projects'n'sundries. Mind tends to wander through the trees up in these elevations. Close enough to the clouds to lose one's head in 'em, I reckon." Joules popped another peppernut into his cheek, tasting at it a bit before crunching it. He gestured towards the calendar in Todd's hand with his fistful of nuts, fat fingers sprinkled with flecks of spice. "Figgered you of all people'd find aught of value in them auguries. Omens and magicks of nature being what and all you claim as yer heritage."

"It was never a choice I would have made freely, believe you me." Todd set the calendar back into its basket, shaking her head before approaching the counter. "Sky signs and tea leaves—doesn't matter when or where you were born, we all get handed the deeds to our lives 'as is'. Nobody ever changed their fortunes because the stars in the sky made it so."

"S'pose that's true," Joules nodded, spitting out some husk fragments. "Then again, nobody ever got lost 'neath the stars if'n they had the sense and wherewithal to read 'em. Guiding principles of existential purpose notwithstanding, a good cartographer ain't never wanted for nothin' in this life."

Todd tapped her fingers against the counter, appraising the bearded old man with a soft smile. "How you been, Joules?"

He gave a half-shrug, looping a sausage-thick finger around his mug of spiced tea. "Seems more the type'a question I oughta be askin' you. Been a few trips around the sun since we last saw you, even before... well, I ain't got cause to remind you."

Todd appreciated the discretion. "I'm doing... alright. Learning to walk on two feet again."

"Damn sight harder than walkin' on four, I'd imagine."

Todd rolled her eyes. "Tell me about it."

Joules spat again. "Some folks rolled through here, claim they saw a big mama grizzly stakin' her claim out by the falls. Claimed they'd seen the fabled 'Forest Guardian' of ancient yore. I presumed then as do I now that ain't the case."

Todd frowned dismissively. "I'd never have let them get close enough to spot me. No, probably that was that younger male trying to poach my territory last season—I sent him packing quick and in a hurry."

Joules nodded. "Figgered as much."

He let the silence cool his tongue between sips of tea, looking Todd up and down with concerned eyes. "How's the other'un doin'? Little girl?"

"Jeanie?" Todd nodded as well, trying to match Joules's congenial energy. "Fine. She's fine. Growing up quick. Healthy—smart, real smart. I was worried there for a while, after..." She trailed off. "Doctor Finch said it's not hereditary, so. That helped put me at ease. With Judd, it was...that was..."

"Pulled a bad hand," Joules finished for her.

Todd gave a weak smirk. "Just born under the wrong stars, I guess."

Joules sighed. "And the man o'the house? How's he been takin' it?"

The question was left unanswered, Todd averting her eyes. She let her attention wander to the collection of candles lining the countertop beside her. "These new?"

Joules didn't press the matter. He tilted his head, giving Todd the go-ahead. "Just set these last week. Give 'em a try."

Todd lifted one between her fingers, the frosted glass-stained burgundy from the wax inside. "Don't mind if I do." She popped the wax seal, putting her nose past the rim and breathing deep. The smell washed over her tastebuds, making her eyes go lidded. "Mmm. Definitely used lennox berries as the base."

"A jumpin' off point." Joules swept some peppernut husks off the counter. "Easy. What else ya got?"

Todd kept at it, letting the scents build and develop behind her nose, giving her palate the full spread. "Pine needles. Arctic poppy. Seems pretty standard fare so far."

"Yeah, yeah. And?"

Todd paused. She wrinkled her forehead thoughtfully, withdrawing the candle long enough to give it another glance before sniffing again. "Huh. Something else in there..."

"No hints. That snifter a'yours ain't need the help."

She narrowed her eyes, searching her mental catalogue of stored scents. It was definitely familiar, she just couldn't quite—

"Honeybrew?"

Joules shook his head, setting down his mug of tea hard enough to spill some. "Hah. And that is why I ain't never takin' no cash bets against you. Closest anybody else ever got was 'mulled wine', dumb bastard."

Todd gave a small curtsy, savoring her small victory. "Got a name for it yet?"

Joules waggled a finger up and down the row of candles. "Figgered I'd give 'em a trial period. Labels are all blank; you're welcome to it if somethin' tickles yer fancy."

Candle

Todd reached over the counter, selecting a red marker from the cup of writing utensils beside Joules. She uncapped it, holding the candle aloft, considering her options. One in particular struck her, and she scrawled a phrase across the label, neat and clean. Capping the marker once more, she set the candle down, rotating it slowly until the label faced Joules. In elegant lettering, it read:

AUGURY OF BEAR

Joules chuffed. "Was hopin' for a one-worder, somethin' that'd take less work to repeat on all 'em labels. Though it'll do for temptin' the tourists, I s'pose."

Todd drew her coat tighter, exhaling long and deep. "It's getting late—I'll have to come back and do my shopping when you're not on your way to closing up. I'll take some of that jerky tonight, though."

Joules scratched his beard, reaching behind the counter to produce a small bundle wrapped in parchment paper. He slid it across the counter, flicking his thumb down across the cashbox as he did, locking the latch. "On the house. Paid for in good conversation."

Todd lifted the bundle, toasting Joules with it before slipping it into her coat. "And good company. Thanks, Joules. Take care of yourself, alright?"

Candle

She turned to leave, her fingers somewhat gritty. The bundle of jerky had some residue clinging to the parchment paper—

*

The withered little shred of meat had been snapped off between someone's teeth, then apparently discarded. They didn't have the taste for appleroot and bison, it seemed. Todd's broad nose nudged the crumpled parchment paper about, sifting the snow around it. Sloppy. They were in too much of a hurry, not concerned about leaving rubbish behind. Each new clue she found was beginning to paint a picture in Todd's mind of her intended target. Matching uniforms, corporate-issued equipment, locally bought rations—these were hired bodies. Paid men, but not professionals, at least not when it came to exploring these woods.

Likely their employer had put them to task without much information to go on beyond their main goal; snatching children was their only concern, why waste time on the other sordid details concerning fey magic and druids?

Todd was nearly through the thicket now—she looked ahead, into the darkness. This may prove a complication. If these hunters weren't confident in their survival skills, and were beginning to lose their nerve as a result of losing one of their own to some forest spirit, they might start to rethink their priorities. If it came down to ensuring their own survival and completing a contract for a dishonest client, they may opt to abandon their captives while making their exit from the forest—or, worse still, dispose of them altogether.

Candle

That couldn't happen. Not on Todd's watch. Not in her forest.

The bear clawed at the snow, tossing the trashed jerky aside. Once more, into the thicket. She was running out of time.

Away

Someone was following her.

Between the trees, in the darkness—dark within dark, figures behind the shadows, flitting between the gaps. Todd hefted her bulk forward, picking up the pace. Whoever it was, they were fast, impossibly so.

No, not someone. Something. Some*things*. Not following—giving chase. The packed ground began to slope downhill, lending Todd the added speed on gravity's behalf, and yet still they matched her pace. Exceeded it, even; there were shadows moving in the dark of the thicket ahead of her. Staying just out of reach, they wanted her to know they were there. Surrounding her.

Faster. Run faster. Todd couldn't afford more delays, more fey spirits attempting to stimulate their egos after centuries of boredom in these shadowlands. She had to outrun the forest itself.

The thicket was drawing tighter, the thicket closing in on her. The forest was growing as fast as she could run, the air itself becoming dense with dread. Her nose betrayed her; she could smell no living flesh, could taste no tang of warm blood pumping through beating hearts. The trees themselves had come alive, and given themselves purpose against her. The thicket had become a wall on either side of her, snapping shut like jaws, tearing into her hide with fanged thorns—

And she was free to the other side, her vision streaked with the blue paint of snow between the black and light. Shrugging away the thorns of the living thicket, Todd spun about on all fours, planting her enormous paws firmly and roaring back her challenge to the concealed spirits.

At first, there was no response. Then, there was the snap of twigs, branches. The bark of the trees began to split apart, spidery limbs emerging from within, unfolding towards her. Todd stood her ground even as what seemed to be more than a dozen carapaces of bark and gnarled branches crept towards her from within the shadows of the thicket—mimics that lived inside and among the trees, wearing their wood as flesh and armor. They had no recognizable faces to speak of, no mouths to speak from, but she knew they were gazing upon her: rising from their branching spinal columns, knotted wood vaguely resembling human skulls, each with a spiral carved into their surfaces that had been stripped of bark. The spirals hummed with resonant sound and dead light alike, acting as both eye and mouthpiece.

One tree mimic stepped forward from the rest, his many branch legs uncoupling themselves from the wooden trunk of his thorax. His faceless visage extended out from his neck, meeting Todd at eye level, and the spiral within his carved veneer began to resonate:

"Reveal yourself, skin-changer. We'll not suffer the indignity of your deceit."

These spirits would not tire, and proved their speed sufficient to outpace Todd no matter how fast she tried to run from them. With every defiant grunt and snort, she obliged, dismissing the larger form of the bear to stand before her captors once more as a human.

"Kill me now or let me go, but don't waste my time trying to impress upon me how you've imagined I trespassed upon you or your land," Todd spat. "This is my land as much as yours—I'm no outsider, and you can't frighten me."

The branches of the mimic creaked as he began to circle Todd, the clawlike ends of his limbs stabbing into the snow like some great arthropod. "All who bleed are outsiders to us. As for fear, we know it not, and cannot give it to you. Invite our displeasure, and the fear you conceal from us may yet be all that remains of you this night."

Todd was unmoved. "Speak your piece, spirit. I have other matters to attend to."

"Matters of life and death, yes." The head of the mimic shuddered, the spirit within quaking as it attuned itself to the emotional state of the mortal it had chosen to converse with. "Always the same. 'Spare' a life. 'Save' a life. I cannot sympathize, for I cannot die. A puzzle: perhaps you can tell me the answer."

He stomped his forelimbs to bring himself to a stop before Todd, the frozen branches crackling at the joints. "Other mortals passed through, this very evening. Three entered the thicket, and two departed. The one who remained was pulled apart beneath our ministrations—he said the most curious thing before his dissolution, repeating an adage we've heard many times before. A request for us to 'make it quick'; borne of fear, disguised as courage."

The mimic snapped his neck towards Todd, his spiral veneer facing her once more. "Why is the quick death what you all seem to crave, despite the sum total of your existence bent on preserving life as long as possible?"

Todd swallowed. Her voice was softer when she replied, knowing the answer all too well. "It's not that we want to die quickly. It's the suffering. We want as little of it as we can stand when we reach the end."

The mimic's head shuddered once more. "A presumption that you have suffered enough in life prior to the end. I would think it a blessing, to die slowly. To die as you live, prospering even in death."

Todd sighed. "And the man you captured? Was his death quick, like he asked?"

The mimic tilted his head. "His death was interesting."

"Well." Todd smiled from behind pursed lips, already testing the limits of her patience. "May I *interest* you with an offer of a quiet night once more, absent the intrusion of anymore... outsiders?"

"I have a better offer."

The mimic twitched, and the others behind him did the same.

*

Through the wide window, Todd had a clear view of the entire surface of the lake. The snowflakes prickled the surface of the black waters, melting as quickly as they fell, giving the lake the appearance of a reptile's dark scales glinting with pinpricks of white light. Though the rest of the lakehouse was made warm and cozy by the firepit in the den, the windows of this gallery made for poor insulation against the winter cold—Todd compensated for this by draping herself and the loveseat she occupied in downy quilts. One in particular she pulled up over her shoulders bore the stitchings of brown bears dancing amidst blue checkered patterns. This same quilt had kept her bed warm through many winters as a child; it very likely did the same for her mother before her.

Before a word was spoken, Todd sensed Niju in the doorway behind her.

"Beef broil in the kitchen," the old matron barked. "Go in and grab a plate, I'm not serving you any in here and letting you ruin my nice linens."

"I'll pass."

Niju didn't relent. "One small plate. C'mon. Or at least have some tack, or a cookie. Eat something. I'm not buying the 'poor me' shit. I cooked you a meal, you'll respect me enough to have some. Else I'm throwing it out, and you with it."

The old woman gone, Todd sighed heavily, poking her toes out from under the quilts. Cold. Gross. She tucked them back in long enough to rub them together, generating some heat, then emerged once more to touch ground. The polished hardwood wasn't quite freezing, but was well on its way—she tiptoed across the room, quickly seeking out the warmth of the thick rug in the next room over.

Timber was here in the den, reclined back in his favorite chair—he had the right idea, his bare feet elevated towards the fire pit. Todd hoped she'd be allowed to pass in peace.

No such luck. "Mom made lunch. It's in the kitchen."

"That's where I'm headed."

"We already ate." Timber shifted in his seat, not making eye contact. "Fixed Jeanie a plate. She's been keeping it down fine—hasn't gotten sick in a few days. Might interest you to know that."

Todd stopped short of the doorway, deciding to hear Timber out against her better judgment. She knew there was no winning when he got like this. "Well, that's good," she finally said, the least combative thing she could think of.

"Yeah, no worries. I'm taking good care of her while you're in there feeling sorry for yourself." He tilted his head, making eye contact with Todd now. "Ever feel sorry for the rest of us? Ever feel anything besides contempt? Or do you just hate your own family that much?"

"I don't *hate*—"

"I know you want me to be this..." Timber stood, hands in front of him, searching for the words. "...Bad guy. I'm not. I'm not the boogeyman you think I am, trying to take your kids away. We come up here because we have to; because you can't take care of Jeanie on your own, and Mom has to take up the slack."

Todd didn't like how Timber had taken to calling his mother-in-law "Mom", but decided against bringing that up just now. "I just don't think we should be trying to dump Jeanie into some institution the minute things get hard for us—"

"It's a good school," Timber argued, continuing the thread from some previous conversation. "She'll have friends, teachers, a sense of community. She'll be out in the real world, away from our antisocial nonsense. She deserves a chance at a normal life."

"A boarding school is not the 'real world', Tim."

"And this is?" Timber spread his arms, looking around. "Raised by a family of self-hating shapeshifters one week, stranded alone in a mountain cabin the next? While her mom goes off and wanders the wilderness, guarding the village against imaginary threats? You're never home, and when you are, you make it clear you don't want to be. Dragging you up here to see Mom is the only way I can convince you to stay human long enough to have a real conversation. With Judd gone, Jeanie doesn't have anyone to look up to, and you're not—"

"Stop, Tim. Just, stop. Just—" Todd clasped her hands together pleadingly. "Give me more time. Let me consider it. Look for other options. Those places don't give kids normalcy, they take it away from them. I just feel like it would be admitting we failed as parents—"

"Maybe we did!" Timber threw his hands up. "Maybe that's exactly what we did. And maybe it's about time we come to terms with that—*you* come to terms with that. I don't know where I went wrong, and you won't tell me, so." He let his arms fall again, shrugging in defeat. "Maybe you need to just...let her go for a while. If more time is really what you think you need, and you would rather run away than be with us, then go. Let me make the decisions you don't want to make."

Todd stood her ground. "I'm not leaving. I belong here. This is my home."

Timber crossed his arms, his gaze narrowing. "No, Todd, I don't think it is. I don't think it ever was."

*

"You will hunt down the other outsiders. The humans who escaped us—they must not leave this land alive."

The mimic rolled his spine back, the wood clicking ominously, his faceless head drawing itself up over Todd to tower over her. "And when it is done, you will leave these woods. You have no place here, outsider, and must return to your mortal world. We've allowed your intrusion to go on long enough."

Todd stood her ground. "I'm not leaving. I belong here. This is my home."

"While there are times we allow those touched by the spirits to find solace here amongst these shadowed trees," the mimic replied, "You have never been welcome. Despite any...self-deceptions you've mistaken for our good graces. I said we would not suffer the indignity of your deceit, and you reveal more than just your true self to us now. We see the conflict, the loyalty to the life you've left behind—you cannot conceal your true desires from us."

Todd faltered, her lip quivering. "Maybe there was a time. When I did want that—to live a world away. As a human. Among other humans. But that was a long time ago. I haven't wanted that for..."

She struggled to think of how much time had passed, living in these woods. "...Many, many years."

The mimic lowered its spidery frame once more. He seemed to wilt somewhat, as if reappraising Todd. Attuned to her emotions, she didn't need to speak for the ancient spirit to see the wounds Todd still nursed deep inside.

"The human hunters you pursue. Your prize—the children they carry with them. Yes?"

Todd nodded. "Yes."

"The children may stay. Return them to their home, and we will allow your safe passage on your return journey. When your righteous work is complete, you must leave, and seek purpose in your life beyond the veil of these woods." The mimic turned away, the others beginning to disappear into the shadows of the thicket once more, melding into the bark and the trunks of the dark trees. "This is the extent of our mercy, and the most charitable we have been towards one of your kind since we were borne into this world. Do not make the mistake of believing yourself welcome anymore. That time has passed."

He paused just long enough to turn, giving one final farewell: "When your time comes, I pray you die slowly, skin-changer."

With the loud cracking of frozen bark, the mimic merged himself with a tree, leaving Todd alone once more.

No riddles, no games, no payments owed. Just a simple ultimatum: leave, or die. The forest had made up its mind, and decided it no longer needed a druid's protection.

Todd spat on the ground defiantly. She had no reason to leave, and would be damned if she was going to let some common woodland spirits force her out.

A lesson left unlearned.

With the mimics gone, the bear trudged on.

Prey

The trees were thinning now, the ground sloping upward. Todd was approaching the foothills of the far mountain, across from where her journey had begun within the shadowed valley. Over or around the mountain, either way meant leaving these woods, and re-entering human lands; the hunters would not brave going over the top in this weather. Around was their only way out before sunrise.

Todd hadn't considered the possibility that she might not catch up before then—the spirits she'd encountered had slowed her progress dramatically. She was beginning to think there was a real chance these intruders might see the end of the forest before they saw the morning sun. A druid like Todd, or another blessed by fey magic, could come and go as they pleased (the imps and troublemaker spirits had Todd to corral them and spare the human world from their mischief). A human or other mortal entering these woods during nighttime would have no choice but to exit once more before morning, or risk being stuck in the shadowlands forever.

The price paid for stealing children. The hunters deserved far worse.

Todd only wondered if she'd make it in time to give it to them.

Bounding through the dense snow, tossing up flurries of white all around, Todd almost missed it; were it not for her sensitive nose, she would have. A nearby conifer, amidst a steep snowbank. There was a dark smear across its bluish bark, visible even in the low light, though Todd didn't need to see it to know it was blood. Her great, bulky frame came to a skidding halt, and she locked in on the scent. Jowls dripping with foamy saliva, Todd panted and licked her chops, smearing the scent across her olfactories and tastebuds alike as her snout prodded at the base of the tree. Human, of course, male. Older, more mature, based on the trace elements of smoke and dark liquor he frequently enjoyed. He also enjoyed a diet of fatty meats and iron-rich vegetables. Todd snuffed about, picking up new details each second she spent analyzing; this was all very rich and flavorful, but she shouldn't have been able to pick up so much detail in this weather. The snow coming down as thick as it was, the temperature so far below freezing, the blood shouldn't have been warm enough for her to be able—

The surface of the tree exploded in her face, Todd lurching back just in time to avoid being blinded by the shrapnel, though she couldn't save her ear from being shredded. Ears ringing. Blood dripping down her neck. The gunshot's report only registered once Todd began bounding away once more, coming from atop the ridge ahead of her. Brassy, deep, with a rolling whip-crack of an echo. Short-barreled, but high caliber. Whatever it was, it wasn't meant for hunting deer or small game. This hunter aimed to kill Todd, and had come prepared, armed with a weapon capable of defending against most anyone.

But Todd was not just anyone.

Slipping between the trees, narrowly avoiding the whip-crack of a second shot that kicked up at her forepaws, Todd put a particularly wide conifer between herself and where she believed the shots were coming from—the bear disappeared behind the tree, and the woman stayed put, flattening herself out of sight against its surface. With any luck, from the hunter's perspective it would appear as if the bear had simply vanished.

She waited, her ear still ringing, chest heaving. A hand went up to feel gingerly at the side of her head: the ear bleed freely, chewed up raw in the blast, but remained attached. It would heal quickly, provided she kept her wits about herself and got herself out of this situation alive.

Todd inhaled deeply, the cold air stinging her lungs, her eyes squeezing shut. She blocked out the pain, the noise, and centered herself. Deep breaths. Calming her pulse, withdrawing inward. Step out into view too soon, she'd be shot. Wait too long, the hunter would escape once more, set up another ambush further on.

She searched herself for a way out. The way through this.

*

"Todd? Did you hear what I said?"

She'd found herself in a daze, staring into the swirling streaks in the grain of Doctor Finch's polished mahogany desk. It felt like the lights had blown themselves out upstairs; there was a ringing in her ears.

"No, I don't think I did." Todd tasted the dry walls of her mouth, her tongue knotting up. "You said...no, I didn't hear what you said. No."

She had heard him. She just didn't accept it.

Doctor Finch had his weight rested forward on the desk, hands folded together. His posture was that of compassion, intent, sincerity. He repeated himself, gently, but with confidence that what was being said must be understood.

"The damage has already been done. My training, my experience in these matters, they are extensive—but within the capabilities of human medicine, we cannot expect a reversal to be possible at this point."

Todd opened her mouth to reply—no sound did she make. She pursed her lips, swallowed. Her insides were a desert. She swallowed again.

"She was getting better." Todd's brow was furrowed so hard she could feel the vein in her temple. "She was out of the woods. She'd cleared the worst of it—you saw. You saw how well she was doing. Now that we know what this is, we can't—?"

She didn't finish the sentence; Doctor Finch's expression said it all. He reached a hand out, taking hers, his callouses scraping her knuckles.

"An illness is one thing. A virus, a parasite—these follow cycles, patterns. We simply caught on to what was happening to her far too late. This kind of substance..." He paused, choosing his words. "So deliberate. Administered in doses, the way it was, at random intervals. If you'd caught him in the act, rushed Jeanie here to the clinic...maybe we could have salvaged some of her major functions, but even that would have been a miracle. Please understand; we weren't fighting Jeanie's sickness, Todd. We were fighting his. And without knowing what he was capable of, we simply had no chance against that kind of... evil."

She felt it coming—the burning behind the eyes. The knot in her throat. Todd held it all back. She fought as hard as she could.

The door behind her clicked open softly, and someone cleared their throat. Finch nodded back at them, then released Todd's hand, standing up. "Give me one moment, dear."

He strode past, cupping her shoulder as he went. Todd looked out the window beyond, watching the blue branches of the conifers turn white in the soft snowfall. She overheard the quiet conversation behind her, even without turning to listen in.

"Did you find him?"

"Not yet. Rover's gone, along with many of their valuables. Coffer was cleaned out. We're still dragging the net, but..."

Todd didn't need to hear Sheriff Yao finish his sentence to know what he was thinking. In these mountains, so far from the rest of the world, Timber could have gone anywhere. He could have thrown a dart at the map, and they'd never find him, not with the limited reach of their village's manpower.

She heard the doctor step out, and the sheriff in. He stopped beside Todd, resting his hand against the back of her chair. She didn't raise her eyes to meet his. The old gunslinger had a nickel-plated two-baller on his hip—for a lightning-quick moment, Todd imagined grabbing it off his belt and putting both barrels in her mouth.

"I'm sure you heard me just now," said Yao. "I understand you've just received some news—I'll do what I can to remain sensitive to that, but I do need to ask you a few more questions, if you're up to answering. I can come back later, but please understand, time is of the essence..."

He trailed off when Todd raised her hand, nodding as she concealed her eyes from him with the other. "I can answer. Go."

"Alright." Sheriff Yao crouched down, his winter jacket trailing on the ground on either side of him as he did, the melting snow dripping onto the carpet. Todd smelled liquor on his breath—he hadn't smelled that way before going to investigate her cabin this morning.

"You say you hadn't been aware of any strange behavior recently—now, perhaps we'd best expand the scope of that question. Weeks, months ago, had there been any changes you noticed? Something overlooked, or something you might have put behind you? Maybe even before Jeanie was showing signs of being sick?"

Todd shook her head, frowning. "He was always so gentle with her," she said. "So kind. With both of them. Judd, when he was alive, he—we both took it hard, losing him. We argued, more than we ever had before, though I suspect no more than any parents would after losing a kid. Sometimes it got rough."

"Rough?" Yao tilted his head. "He ever—?"

Todd quickly shook her head, raising an eyebrow. Yao nodded in understanding. "Ah. Right." Unwise to put your hands on a woman who could tear you in half.

Yao scratched at the stubble on his neck. "You know, maybe that's something we should explore. Help build us a profile on him. Good dad, tried his best to provide, even if he didn't always succeed—loved his kids, at least out in the open where we could see. He may have resented you, quietly, for what you were capable of. How that made him feel, the man of the house, married to someone who exceeded him in all the ways we—" Yao gestured at the tattoos on his muscled arms. "—How us guys, I mean. How we like to think or present ourselves as being the tough ones, the ones in charge of things. I'm not saying he didn't love you or the kids. Just, maybe he couldn't get past being the smaller person, years married to someone with your ability, your reputation."

"Sheriff. I appreciate that you want to...try to explain what he did, why he did it," Todd said, shaking her head, chin quivering violently. "But I never saw that in him. Years of marriage, I never sussed it out. And I know you want to make me feel better, and put him in the crosshairs..."

She patted a hand against her chest. "But this is on me. This is my failure. I let Jeanie down. And I'm paying for it."

Yao turned his eye down to his boots, sighing heavily.

"These kinds of people," he finally said, after a long pause. "These... hunters. Predators. They aren't always gonna let you see them coming. In fact, more'n half the time, that's their whole strategy; outlast, wait you out. They get in close, close enough to wound, and convince you there's no way out. The really successful ones, the real killers? They'll thrive on less. They'll make you think you hold all the power, that you're the one neglecting them, hurting them. They'll bleed themselves before ever laying a finger on you. But that's what makes them so dangerous: if they're willing to hurt themselves just to sell themselves on a reason to hate you, biding their time, stewing in that misery..."

Yao shook his head.

"Todd, it wasn't your fault. This is on him. Always has been."

He stood, hand on his hip, hovering just above his double-barreled pistol. The two-baller glinted in the yellow light of Finch's candle sconce.

"I'm going hunting. Now, in accordance with the authority the people of this mountain have entrusted me with, policy and procedure dictate that I inform the victim to standby while we conduct our investigation. While we handle things ourselves."

Todd watched Yao's hand carefully as he spoke. The distance he so carefully kept, avoiding touching the weapon at all costs.

"That's exactly how I intend to handle this situation," he continued, "With the next mother I have to have this talk with. Any other woman sitting in this chair, anyone else on the planet? That's exactly what I'd be telling them right now."

Todd raised her head finally, making eye contact with the sheriff.

"And me?"

Yao stiffened. He cleared his throat unconvincingly, straightening his tie. He was the one to avoid eye contact next, looking out the window himself now.

"Don't have many guys to spare on this," he said. "We'll do our best, of course. Don't get me wrong. Soon as I leave this room, I'm going hunting."

He stood rooted to the spot. Not budging an inch.

Todd turned to look over her shoulder.

The door was ajar.

She collected her thoughts, wiping her eyes once more. Then stood. She thought of thanking the sheriff, but decided against it— best not to speak such things aloud, where they could be remembered and regretted later.

Prey

Todd slipped through the open door, the sheriff remaining in the office, not following her out.

Yao was an honorable man, and a decent hunter—in his prime, Todd wouldn't have dismissed the idea that he might have been able to track down Timber himself. He wasn't staying behind because he didn't think himself up to the task.

Todd knew the sheriff better than that, after all these years.

He was simply giving her a head start.

*

Todd's eyes opened slowly, the white glint of snowflakes clinging to her eyelashes turning the world into a crystalline haze before her.

The hunter's blood did not smell of cowardice. It was indulgent, self-assured, confident. He would not be the type to take a shot and run—he would stay put, wait for the next shot, put the beast down. Failing that, he'd move in close for the kill, denying himself nothing but the time spent waiting through his impatience.

She didn't have to get close to him to put him down. She just needed to lure him in close to her.

At the base of the tree she was hiding behind, a thick cluster of bushes had grown together. Little candy red specks were peeking through the dusting of snow covering the bush—ibex berries. Quickly, Todd formulated the ruse in her mind, shrugging off one of her animal pelts and tying two ends of it together to form a makeshift pouch—or at least, give it the appearance of one that had been torn open. She knelt down and quickly began dragging her fingers through the reedy branches of the bushes, scraping off berries by the handful and dumping them into the animal skin. When she'd collected enough, she scattered the final handfuls of berries into the snow away from her, letting the pelt fall into a messy heap.

"Help!" She began crying out, pinching her throat to simulate the vocal fry of someone in distress. "Someone, help! Bear! Wild bear! Come quick!"

Todd sat back against the tree, and waited. Her fingers and palms were slick with bright red berry juice—she splashed some against her neck and chin, just enough to make it seem like she'd suffered some minor injury.

The seconds ticked past. Minutes. She waited still, quietly, making herself as small as possible at the foot of the tree. She held her breath, straining her lungs.

Then, she heard it—the snow crunching, footfalls approaching at a metered pace. Apprehensive, but not suspicious. Good.

"Hello? You there, miss?"

Todd let out a mock gasp, letting herself breathe again, quick and sharp—she needed to sound frightened, out of breath. Peeking around the tree, she saw the dark silhouette of a man, several yards away—ducking back out of sight, Todd sobbed, arm outstretched to wave him in closer.

"Hurry, hurry! If you run, you can catch up to it! It went just thataway!"

The hunter picked up his knees, rushing forward into view, his back to Todd. He took a few steps more, his stubby rifle raised in anticipation, but seemed to think better of it as he halted.

"No sense chasing after it if I got no bead on it," he grumbled. "Must've slipped away. Dammit—shouldn'ta let it outta my sight."

Todd stabbed a finger out, waving it around at no direction in particular. "No no, if you run quick, it went that way! I saw it, it took a swipe at me, your shot scared it off—!"

"Ahh, naw, it's long gone." The hunter shook his head, turning heel to face Todd. His face was mostly obscured by his scarf and goggles, his shaggy mustache and ruddy cheeks the only identifying features Todd could make out. "You injured? Said it took a swipe at you, yeh?"

Todd stood to her feet, shaky—she rubbed her hands together nervously, showing her red palms. "I just—only a little scrape," She stuttered, wiping at her shoulder. "Looks worse than it really is, I'm sure. I was out late, strayed a little too far, got caught in the storm while gathering berries for my famous Midwinter Pie..."

The hunter chuffed, throwing the rifle back over his shoulder. "Midwinter Pie—famous, you say? Ain't sure I ever had it before." He took a moment, sizing Todd up. She hoped they were close enough to the edge of the forest that her story held water—he'd never buy that she was anything but another trickster spirit if they were still deeper into the shadowlands.

The lie seemed to hold true. He stepped forward, raising a gloved hand—Todd could see a slash mark running across his forearm. Likely suffered the injury when escaping the mimics, using the subsequent bleed to set his trap for her. "Name's Downsey. I'm a—well, let's just say contractor, out on a job. You know, you really shouldn't be out in these woods, this is real dangerous territory—and I'm talkin' more than just bears and the like."

Todd nodded, giving a nervous giggle as she shook Downsey's hand. "Yeah, tell me about it—I grew up there," she said, waving in the general direction behind her. "Just on the other side of this mountain, little fishing village on the river—maybe you...?"

"Ah, yeah, we spent the past night there just before heading into these woods." Downsey shrugged his other shoulder, a heavy-looking pack of some kind slung across his back. "Well, this weather looks like it'll last the night entire, if you need an escort out of these woods, my friends and I..." He cleared his throat. "...Friend, and I. Well, we're heading back that way, we can lead you out, if'n you'll have us as company. I ask to be polite, but frankly I'd have to insist, on account of the aforementioned dangers."

Todd stepped in close, nodding, keeping her eyes big and wide. As vulnerable as she could make herself seem, that was the play. "Oh surely? I'd be so thankful for that—I'd have to reward you boys with some of that pie." She peeked around his back, trying to get a better look at the pack he was carrying. "Speaking of, I haven't had much but berries to eat since before sundown, I don't suppose—"

Downsey quickly stood up straight, taking a step back to keep the pack away from Todd. In that moment, she could almost swear she saw it move. "No rations to speak of, I'm afraid," he said quickly, sounding nervous. "Just camping equipment and the like, we ate all we had a ways back. But I'd be much obliged to take you up on that offer for pie—the quicker we get out of these woods, the better, yeh?"

Todd nodded demurely. "Of course, Mister...Dew...Down..."

"Downsey, yeah," he chuckled, his grin permanently affixed across his flushed face. Todd wasn't quite flirting with him, but ditzy definitely seemed to be his type.

"Downsey," she repeated. "Lead the way, then."

Flask

Bodies filtered out of the tiny chapel's doors, the mourners all raising their hands and hats to shield themselves from the rainwater dripping off the awning overhead. The sun seemed to hide itself away behind the gray clouds and the tops of the trees, ashamed to greet the late morning after the night's rain. Todd felt much the same, standing alone outside the chapel, forgetting to even change into the expected black clothes everyone else had worn to Jeanie's service. Instead, she still wore the same mustard brown coat she'd worn on her trek into the woods the night before—it was the only outerwear in her wardrobe that hadn't been gifted to her by Timber. He was the one who had introduced her to the habits of fashion in 'normal' human women, as Todd had spent her whole life used to the idea that she could simply shift into a bear anytime she was cold.

Wearing black to a place like this was something she'd only done once before, and hadn't yet learned to make a habit of it, as other humans did. She suspected living the short lives they did meant the gesture meant more to them than she'd yet come to appreciate—it all just seemed so performative.

Doctor Finch and his wife passed her by, the good doctor nodding his condolences. Todd nodded back stiffly. It wasn't that she blamed him, only that she'd never had a conversation with the man that didn't end in bad news.

Niju was next to make eye contact. The old matron wore a black shroud that trailed behind her—she was clearly more used to these human ceremonies than her daughter. She looked Todd in the eye, briefly, then away again. She didn't even bother speaking a word as she passed. Todd may have been conflicted on where the blame lay for what happened to Jeanie, but she knew Niju didn't have a shred of doubt on who deserved to fall on the sword.

She suspected this might be the last time she saw her mother. Maybe it was for the best.

The small crowd dispersed, and the last two approached Todd directly—Sheriff Yao and Joules, the shopkeeper. They both wore matching suits, and Todd didn't doubt they were both borrowed from the tailor across the lane from Joules's shop.

"Marm," Joules said, and the two men both bowed slightly as they stood before Todd.

Todd nodded back. "I suspect the rest of these fine people will have a lot to say about how the girl's own mother couldn't be bothered to attend the funeral."

Yao shook his head. "Don't pay them any mind. We understand completely. You've done a lot for our little community since you first moved in—you don't own anyone an explanation. We're grateful to you and all your family, truly."

Todd flexed her eyebrows. "Mm. Don't think the feeling is mutual as far as Niju is concerned, but I'd say to take your own advice as far as she's concerned."

Joules reached forward, his fat fingers cupping at Todd's elbow. "Most the world gotten used to the spirits and the wonders— made peace with yer kind'n'all others what been touched by magic. Li'l outposts like ours, away from the big Houses'n'territ'ries, we ain't all caught up with the modern world. Some'a us humans ain't even seen a beastman, let alone shapechangers what kin wear their skins at their leisure."

"Something like this," Yao added, pointing his thumb back at the chapel, "They think this is all they have to look forward to— their final reward, a goodbye from friends and family who gather on their behalf. Small-minded, can't imagine what it must be like for someone like you, a few steps down the ladder from being immortal."

Todd nodded again, gazing off into the distance. "I appreciate you guys trying to make me feel understood, but the truth of it is I simply forgot what day it was. I missed the service, plain and simple. Nothing deeper than that. Another failure on my part."

Yao bowed his head slightly once more. "I wish you wouldn't see it like that, Todd. We certainly don't. If this is on you, that means it's on all the rest of us, too—none of us saw through his act. Ask anyone in town, they'd have said he was just a loving father looking after his family."

Todd looked to Joules, making a beckoning motion with her hand. Taking her meaning, he reached into his suit, withdrawing a small leatherbound flask from his inner pocket. "Where there's smoke, there's fire," he warned, handing the flask over, "Take it slow—this is from a barrel of some disrepute 'mongst the pub crowd."

"Sounds perfect."

Todd uncapped the flask and took a pull, long and deep. It was definitely smokey, and definitely burned like spitfire all the way down—if she had any tears left in her, she'd have gone blurry-eyed. She handed it back, suppressing a cough in her throat. "Fuck me. You weren't kidding."

Joules offered the flask to Yao, who looked around, making sure no one saw as he accepted. "Supposed to have cut out the hard stuff years ago. My wife finds out I haven't been on the wagon since last Midsomer, she'll have my balls for pearls."

He took a quick pull, snorting through his nose as it hit. "Goddamn, that your daily drink?"

Joules accepted the flask back, shrugging. "Only afore noontimes." He tipped it back, draining the flask before pocketing it once more, wiping his beard clean. "You headin' back, I take it?" He asked Todd.

Todd squinted, looking uncomfortable. "I actually meant to ask—you still have that room above the shop made up for when the inn is full?"

Joules nodded. "Li'l dust, I expect that ain't hurt it none. Welcome to it, as long as ya like."

"I would like." Todd looked back to the chapel once more. "I don't know if I'm ready to go inside just yet. Couldn't go in the house, either—it's like this whole village is closing its doors to me, one by one. Like all the warm and welcome is being choked out."

Yao clasped his hands together apologetically. "You've lost more than your fair share, Todd, but you will always be welcome here. Our doors will be open to you forever. Whether you choose to continue living among us, or look for something else back where you came from—it makes no difference to us. Cherrystone is famous for its bear of legend, now. You brought tourism back to these mountains, not to mention all the poachers you've dealt with."

"We're indebted to our graves and beyond," Joules agreed. "Which I suspect is closer to the truth than a simple turn a'phrase, given yer purported longevity and whatnot."

Yao took a step back. "I'll handle things here. You can visit Jeanie behind the chapel in your own time, Todd—go with Joules back to the shop, I'll meet you two for drinks later. Real drinks, I mean, not that engine degreaser."

"Engine d'greaser is real drinks," Joules argued, watching Yao go.

He chuckled, looking back to Todd. "We hoofin' it?"

Todd waved him on. "Lead the way."

*

"Here."

Downsey had taken the lead, and had stopped in his tracks to offer his flask back to

Todd. "It's somethin' strong and fierce, so a little waif like yourself might get knocked outta your pants, but it should help warm you up if nothin' else about it appeals."

Todd accepted the flash, uncapping it and maintaining unblinking eye contact with Downsey as she slugged it back, quaffing off the entirety of the flask's contents in a single go. Wiping her lower lip, she handed the flask back, leaving Downsey dumbstruck as he weighed the empty vessel in his hand.

"Well shit, lady, good thing I filled up on the cheaper stuff."

She nodded, raising an eyebrow. "I can tell."

Downsey cackled, stuffing the flask back into his heavy coat. "I knew I liked you."

When he turned away once more, the oversized pack on his back shifted, and Todd's eyes locked on. There was something moving inside, definitely, though in human form she couldn't pick up the scent of what. One of the cubs, maybe. If she were being optimistic, both. Not a safe bet as far as the hunters were concerned, leaving only one of their troupe to carry both prizes on his back, especially considering the proven odds of getting split up from each other. Todd decided to have a try at pulling information from Downsey as they trudged on.

"You made a point to correct yourself earlier," she began, keeping a light and curious tone. "You said 'friends', then 'friend', like there's only two of you where used to be..."

"Four," Downsey finished ruefully. "I wasn't having fun with you when I said this place is dangerous. Fuckin' woods ate us up, and the two of us left got separated after the last encounter with an... well, let's say an unfriendly creature. Couldn't put a name to it if I tried."

How thoughtful of him—he was being condescending enough to Todd's sensibilities to spare her the gory details. "What were you hunting, if you don't mind me asking?"

Downsey slowed slightly, his head tilting—Todd mentally cursed herself, preparing a course correction as he spoke again. "I never said we were hunting..."

"Of course not, I only assumed with the heavy weaponry and whatnot," Todd quickly offered. "People don't usually come around these mountains loaded for bear unless they're... loaded for 'bear', you know?"

"Hah. Good one." Downsey shrugged, adjusting the heavy pack. "Yeah, s'pose that's fair enough. I shouldn't be telling a stranger too much of this, considering it was a privately funded venture and all, but after the shit night I've had, well..."

Todd waited, giving him room to consider. Better she didn't push her luck with constant questioning. Her patience paid off.

"The four of us work for the Angilas Institute," Downsey began. "I don't suppose you've heard of us?"

"Mm-mm."

"Yeah, I'll save you the boring details, then. Basically, we work contract research, get

our funding from private grants and clientele—
they provide the backing and the leads, we
provide the manpower and do all the fieldwork.
Usually the boring stuff; geological samples
here, map a pack of nihiloraptor migration
patterns there. Every once in a while, though, a
client puts out a real exciting contract. A job
that gets us close to, well... the other side."

"The other side?"

Downsey grinned back at her. "Magic.
The occult. The real freaky shit. Now I'm not
sayin' I believe one way or another half the stuff
people make claims on, I'm a scientist at heart.
Most 'magic' I've seen in life ended up bein' little
more than unexplained biological phenom, or
at the very least, some very impressive parlor
tricks. Every so often though, you come across a
place you can't really explain away so easy... like

these woods. Spooky place. Strange things been happenin' ever since we set foot in 'em..."

Oh please. Todd found her mind beginning to wander as the naïve hunter went off on his campfire tale tangent. Wasn't bad enough that Downsey had all the charisma of a smooth boulder, but now Todd had to follow along and pretend to be mystified by his salesman pitch on a subject she knew infinitely more about than he ever would.

She had to find a way to get him back on track, and find out more about the remaining hunter. And fast—if she wanted to keep her sanity intact.

"Oh!" Todd stumbled suddenly, falling to her hands and knees in the snow. "Oh, no, oh shit... I'm sorry, I just... suddenly feel so faint..."

Downsey about-faced, rushing over to kneel before Todd. "Is it your injury acting up? Still bleeding real bad?" He set his rifle down in the snow, letting his hands roam over Todd's neck and torso, searching in vain for her wounds.

Todd nodded letting her eyelids flutter. "Yes, please, if you have anything—some salves, or an adjuvant of some kind..."

"Nah, my buddy is the one with all the medical supplies," Downsey said. "Afraid I can't help you out until we catch up. Should be just over that rise there." He pointed in the direction they were headed.

"Over that rise?"

"Uh-huh. We set up base camp in a little cave, on the southwestern slope of the mountain."

"Southwestern slope. And the other hunter's name?"

"Hm?" Downsey turned back. "Oh. Travers."

"Travers. Thanks."

Her hands were lightning fast as she stood up, bringing the discarded rifle up directly into the underside of Downsey's chin with a powerful crack. The older man teetered on his feet before slumping sideways in the snow, knocked out cold.

Todd pointed the rifle down at the unconscious man's head, watching carefully for any signs of resurgence. Blood trickled out of the corner of his mouth, but otherwise he remained still.

"Finally," she sighed. She doubted he was ever planning on revealing their true purpose for being in these woods—not that she needed to know more than she already did, anyway. Didn't matter the reason; taking children was sufficient motivation for her to give chase.

Speaking of.

Todd rolled Downsey over onto his belly, facing his heavy pack now. Leaning down once more, she felt a twinge of premature relief as she found the pack's fastener. If indeed both children were inside, she'd save herself the last leg of her journey to the forest's edge. These men had proven themselves unprepared for the shadowlands—even if she let the last hunter go free, the odds were still against him he'd make it out before sunrise.

Still. She couldn't get ahead of herself. She had to be sure.

Holding her breath, Todd unclasped the fastener, lifting the pack's flap open.

There was a bundle of cloth, soft, warm—a blanket. Something was stirring within.

Todd began peeling back the layers, the green blanket slightly dewy beneath her fingers: condensation from someone's breathing. Someone small. Someone...

Todd froze. It was someone's child, sure enough.

Fleshy, smooth scales, a reptilian hide of dark blue with bright red stripes. An underbelly of creamy white, little clawed hands bundled into dozy fists, jammed into the little creature's saurian snout as it suckled.

It was not one of Wolfmother's cubs. This was neither human, nor druid.

A kuaneach child, just barely hatched. A dragonfolk.

Todd scoffed, shaking her head. Just her luck. She went looking for what should have been easy prey, and found herself a mystery. Someone *else's* child to be returned. But no kuaneach lived in these woods—hell, Todd hadn't even seen a kuaneach come anywhere near these mountain ranges as long as she lived. She'd only met one or two in her lifetime the few times she'd ventured out to the bigger cities in the House territories.

"And just who are you supposed to be?" Todd asked rhetorically.

The sleeping infant didn't respond, naturally. Todd wondered if this might be a chemically induced sleep—would make sense, all things considered. Even at a young age, some kuaneach were capable of impressive violence. At first glance, Todd assumed the child to be male, though she didn't want to stake too much on that assumption given her limited exposure to the species. More important than that was the child's origin: wherever it came from, it was not these woods, meaning either Downsey's troupe had brought the infant in with them...

Or, more likely, and more troubling, had simply found it.

"Fuck." Todd shook her head, watching the little draconic child snooze. "And here I thought I was getting close to finishing my work for the night."

The little dragonkin burbled quietly, and Todd pulled the blanket over its head once more, ensuring it stayed warm. Closing the pack, Todd stood, staring down with disgust at the unconscious Downsey. These men truly had no shame.

Nor did she, as for a moment of self-doubting horror, Todd actually found herself considering leaving the pack behind as she went on ahead. This wasn't her child, wasn't her responsibility.

Then again, neither were Wolfmother's cubs.

In for a penny, in for a pound.

"Fine." Todd stuffed the stubby rifle into one of the outer pouches, then gripped the pack and yanked. Hard. She wriggled it up and off of Downsey's shoulders, silently wishing she dislocated one of his arms in the process. The pack was indeed heavy, though nothing she couldn't handle, even in human form. Loosing the straps as much as they were capable of, Todd looped her arms in, and began to shift—in bear form, she'd need as much slack as possible to accommodate her added bulk.

A few moments later, the bear shuffled her great forelimbs in place, adjusting the pack on her wide back so it was as snug and secure as possible. She had a lot of ground to cover, and needed to do so, fast—it wouldn't do to have the kuaneach infant slipping off.

Todd looked to Downsey one final time. Even if he posed a threat to her at this point, there was no way he'd be able to catch up to her before she reached the mountain.

No sense in hanging back any longer. The woods would decide what to do with him.

Todd aligned herself towards the mountain, and set off on her final approach, beginning her ascent up through the foothills— mystery child in tow.

Abandon

Todd couldn't bring herself to enter the cabin. Try as she might, the idea of taking one step closer to those stairs that led up to the porch—she might as well be trying to pull her own teeth out. The homestead had lost all allure, all sense of comfort and welcome, standing down as a dark gravestone marking the site of her own failure. The windows had frosted over, nothing but darkness visible from within. No warm meal awaited her, no candles lit to light her way down the halls, no radioplays coming from Judd's room or sounds of Jeanie's plastic toys clinking together in the den.

She remembered getting a whiff of Timber's favorite honeyed mead in the liquor cabinet by their shared bookshelf and felt sick to her stomach. Every sensory memory, every smell and sight and touch—every inch of that cabin was tainted now. Stained by the black ink that had been spilled across the scrapbook of her memories she'd spent carefully cultivating, here in this once-sacred place. This home, this decision to live a life apart from her mother, from her heritage and inherited purpose. She had never wanted to marry another druid, she had never wanted to raise children in the wilderness, away from the world of humans she loved so much.

Todd just stood there. She'd cried herself to the point of dehydration, her face carved in stone as she glared up those steps, at that front door to her former home.

She couldn't live here. Not now, not ever again. This was a mausoleum, and to stay here would be tantamount to interring herself.

Hours passed on a stiff breeze. Todd began to drift with the winds, in no particular direction. Away from here. Towards anywhere else. The trees grew dense around her, rain and melted snow dripping on her head and shoulders, clothes melting away into the thick pelt of the grizzly. She wandered for miles; up the mountain slopes, across streams, into half-melted snowbanks. It wasn't until the morning sun began to breach the tree canopy, she realized she'd marched all through the night, guided by scent as well as if by sight. When the next morning eclipsed the night, and the hunger pangs began to set in, Todd set to disposing the corpse of a recently shot deer—left behind by some careless hunter who hadn't bothered to pursue the poor creature while it bled out. Ordinarily, Todd would have tracked the scent of the killer and gotten satisfaction from correcting his wasteful ways.

Now, she simply ate for nourishment, and went on her way, as satisfied as any wild bear would be. The desire to look upon another human was absent from her, in its place a benumbed expectation of the coming winter. Hibernating was never in her nature, not while she could live in a warm cabin instead—she might like to have died in the snow instead. The storms were always a fearsome ordeal this side of the mountain. With any luck, she'd starve, a frozen husk of herself, only thawed in the late spring when the sun shifted in the skies to look upon the northern slopes again. This novel thought made weeks disappear in the blink of an eye, and one particularly grey afternoon saw Todd leaving tracks in the snow that rose high enough to reach her knees. The first of the unmelting snow that would last the remainder of the season.

The gift of the druid came with its downsides. No matter how deeply she immersed herself in the role of a wild animal, no matter how much of the bear she let take over, Todd never lost touch with her human soul within. She thought perhaps in exile, she might simply fade away, the dulled intelligence of a beast entombing her rational thought within. But the memories never vanished, and neither did her sense of self—if anything, isolation seemed to focus it, crystalizing the memories in a transparent sheen. The moments of her life that she dreaded the most revisited her one by one, filling the void where the unthinking animal operated her body in her mental absence. The deeper into herself Todd drew, the more of herself she rediscovered.

And yet, wandering through a world of her own painful memories seemed somehow so much more appealing than returning to the real world to make new ones. She'd already survived these moments the first time around, after all.

So, she allowed herself to be folded into the years, bidding spring goodbye to welcome the next winter, never straying beyond the reach of the coldest peaks and thickest forests. At some point Todd became vaguely aware that she'd long since trekked beyond the far reaches of her territory, Cherrystone and its humble trappings an entire world away at this point. No doubt other bears would fill the void she left, taking up residence among the fringes of the outpost, offering tourists that passed through the area a glimpse of what they would swear was the Great Bear of local legend herself.

Todd didn't mind. She simply exited her life, and the lives of all she knew, entering the fugue state of self-imprisonment that wiped away the calendar years like nothing. A prison that followed her all the way into the outermost reaches of the shadowed forests, where humans never dared to tread.

In this valley, the sun never quite reached its zenith overhead, always seeming to hide just out of sight behind the mountains and the ancient loquewood conifers. Where time didn't matter, and the morning crow of a robin may become the soft hoot of a predatory owl in the span of a single breath. More importantly, the most curious thing happened the moment Todd passed into these lands: the memories that encased her spirit all seemed to fizzle away into a fog, turning to wet mist that receded into the corners of her waking mind.

Todd found herself staring at the trunk of a pine tree, the morning sun just barely peeking through the branches above, dappled light shining upon a strange carving of a spiral in the tree's bark. Left by some traveler or long-deceased resident of these woods, Todd didn't know. In fact, the more she stared at the spiral, attempting to recall some meaning behind it, the less meaning she desired to glean from it.

She'd lost interest in symbols and texts, in the idea of leaving sign. In communication. Connecting with anyone at all, in this moment or across time, was a novel idea Todd lacked as a requirement—she simply wasn't there anymore. The bear turned away from the strange spiral, finding she didn't care about the person or idea or passion behind it. It was simply scratchings on a tree.

A tree that, otherwise, was no different than the next, in a forest of thousands; large enough to shield Todd for a thousand lifetimes from the memories that lurked just outside their shadowy fringes.

In this place, maybe she might finally be allowed to forget it all, and simply be Todd.

*

She had arrived.

The cave was a short trek across a rocky outcropping, the larger black stones peeking out from beneath the blanket of snow. Todd sniffed at the air tentatively, discerning no obvious traps lying in wait for her. It seemed well and true she'd come to the end of her journey—or, midpoint, rather. She'd still need to make the trip back, though with the sky turning from speckled black to a deep purple, threatening to go blue, Todd knew the dawn was fast approaching. The morning sun would not be far behind, and would serve to banish the more troublesome spirits until next nightfall. Plenty of time for her to retrace her path to Wolfmother's hut.

The huge grizzly took a careful step forward, then another, keeping her massive weight on her hind legs as she descended into the outcropping. It was a short slope, but just perilous enough to pose a hazard to her footing.

She took it slow and steady, claws digging through the snow to find solid rock to plant her paws against; no sense in coming all this way just to break a leg from being impatient and careless.

A slurry of snow splashed nearby. Todd paused her descent, tracing the source of the sound back to a branch overhead—it wobbled slightly, having been recently disturbed, as if by a bird taking flight.

No matter. Todd took another step, then another, finding her weight level out naturally along with the stones beneath her paws. Eventually she was standing on flat ground again, and she took a moment to shuffle her shoulders, readjusting the pack on her back. Then, she continued on, plodding quietly to avoid alerting anyone who may be lurking near the entrance to the cave.

"Aye, siwmae! I don't suppose ye've any pretty new trinkets in that sack there? I cannae recall ye carryin' such a heavy load when last we traded pleasantries."

Todd withered inside, the bear loosing an impatient snort. She looked up, easily locating the piebald raven on his perch, bright feathers framed against the early morning sky. He preened at himself coolly, like a socialite adjusting the smock of his coat, smoothing out any wrinkles that might tarnish his cultivated appearance.

"Would ye mind terribly if'n I requested your more personable side make an appearance? Much as I'm loathe to follow suit, afraid my Bearish is just mingin'. Would be like listenin' to an old geezer part ways with his innards."

Todd knew there was little choice to be had here, and ignoring the tengu would not end well for her, especially after deferring their last meeting. So, after a few moments, she stood before him as a human once more, slipping the pack off her shoulders to place it on the ground just behind her feet.

"I was just thinking about you," she lied, "And our little game earlier. I'm pretty close to solving that riddle, I think."

"Ach, nae worries there, lass," Cornell said with a wave of his wing. "I've all but forgotten meself. That's a concern for our future selves to address. I've actually come up with a new way to entertain meself—see, when I saw you'd left that last bloke alive—"

"You've been following me this whole time, then?"

Cornell coughed. "Manners. You left him alive, and here I was under the sum impression you'd served these woods as a proper guardian of sorts. All brash and bold, bangin' your way through those trees like a mad bull chargin' down those poor bastards. Me, I took the first, and those shifty treefolk had their way with the second—the third, I'd've swore you'd have skinned for supper. Yet I find you sharin' a drink with the walking blood sausage, leaving him in the cold for summat other to finish him off! You've been mitchin'."

"I assure you, I haven't," Todd rebuked. "He'll be heading this way as soon as he comes around, and once I finish my business in this cave, I'll be going back the way I came—our paths are bound to cross again eventually."

"Mayhaps," Cornell mused, nodding. "Mayhaps not. Maybe mayhaps Marm made me make a mess of the man meself, maybe."

Todd winced. "Don't do that again."

"Irregardlessness," Cornell continued, ignoring her, "I thought it might be a question of motivation—being banished from this realm by the treefolk, owing tribute to yours truly under threat of losing one's very soul... I cannae imagine ye've been made fully aware of just how copper fucked you are. So, the merciful sort I am, I came up with a new game for us to play. A test, of sorts: to see what sort of fire burns in ye what has ye blowin' so much smoke my way. Just another small delay at the end of your path to victorious delivery of the wolf cubs from their degenerate captors. In fact, once I've filled you in on the rules of this little game, I'd be right chuffed if I were ye—the odds are stacked so high in your favor, it's not even fair!"

Todd knew well enough to know this wouldn't be as easy as the raven made it sound. "Don't you have anyone else in these woods to harass? Any other, more worthwhile games to play instead?"

"Nope!" The raven shifted on his branch in excitement. "Ya ready? I know you are. So! This game requires two parties to play, but sadly, I've not the eligible disposition for this particular bout. So, we'll be requirin' the assistance of a third..."

Cornell raised a wing, and Todd felt the hairs on her neck prickle. She turned in time to see someone step out from behind a tree, one far too slender to have concealed his presence naturally. The man wore the same heavy coat and gear as Downsey and the other hunters— the fourth member of their party. He was breathing heavily, his eyes lidded, staring cross-eyed at Todd. He was a passenger in his own body, a puppet on Cornell's invisible strings, unable to resist the pull of the tengu's powerful magicks.

"Meet the mutual thorn in our sides, the human known as 'Travers', and the last little hop-skip you'll need to put beneath and behind you in order to reach your goal and save the kiddies! Say hello, Travers."

Like a ghost had gripped his arm by the wrist, Travers waved at Todd, hand flopping about limply. He let out a weak groan, the most resistance he was capable of.

"Now, Travers, listen carefully, as the rules of this game are equally important to your success as to our ursine friend here. Are we ready to receive?"

Cornell's invisible hand forced Travers to nod. Todd craned her neck back, glaring up at Cornell with visible disgust. "Just get on with it already."

"As you wish!"

Travers stumbled, coughing and gasping for air, as if he'd been holding his breath this whole time. He looked about, getting his bearings, the man clearly in control of his faculties once more. Making eye contact with Todd, he stepped forward, hands outstretched as he began pleading desperately:

"Help me, miss, please, don't let him take me again—he gets in your head, makes you his plaything—he—I—please—puh—"

Travers shuddered violently, his eyes clenching shut before he gripped both sides of his head, letting loose a horrific shriek of torment. Todd stepped backwards, pulling the pack with her, watching the dreadful scene that unfolded before her, the man's scream rising in pitch and frenzy as his neck snapped back with a wrenching twist—

Eat

The bottle's twist-top popped off with a wet puff of foam, Todd laughing as she leaned against the bar for support and accepted the bottle of ale from her companion. "What—" She snorted, composing herself, cheeks flushed as she suppressed her laughter. "What did you say your name was again?"

"Oh, forgotten already, have we?" The taller man guffawed, taking a pull at his own bottle and shaking his head. "Must not be making as much of an impression as I'd hoped."

"Well, until you've heard me calling out your name over and over, you'll have to get used to my poor memory," Todd joked. "Best way to commit someone to memory."

He was as stunned as she was, taking a beat before bursting into laughter along with her once more. Todd couldn't believe her own ears—she never talked like this, not even in her younger years.

"Clay," the man said, extending a hand. "You can call me Clay. Nice to meet you again, Miss..."

Todd stuttered. "I... can't remember!"

Their laughter resumed, Todd's cheeks burning hot as she took a swig. She wasn't even on her fourth—no, fifth bottle, what had gotten into her? Had it really been so long without human contact?

"Okay, Miss 'Can't Remember,' that's gonna be a little hard for me to call out over and over," Clay chuckled, then hesitated. "I don't mean to say I'm assuming anything, just tryin' to go along with it..."

"Shut up, you're fine," Todd encouraged, giving Clay a gentle shove. "You're on the right track. Just gotta check off the few requisite boxes still left. You haven't even asked what I do for fun or for a living, yet."

"With any luck," Clay said between sips, "They'll be the same answer. You don't strike me as the schoolteacher type..."

Todd leaned against the bar, propping her head up with the flat of her palm. "You got something against schoolteachers?"

"Yes, I do," Clay declared proudly, slamming down his bottle. "Yeah, this one time, I threw out an answer without raisin' my hand first, got whacked upside the head with a ruler."

"You poor thing."

"I know, I know," Clay nodded solemnly. "Completely reshaped the curvature of my skull. It's how I got this impressive chin."

"No kidding, lookit the size of it," Todd said in awe, reaching out to press her thumb to it. "Talk about icebreakers; you could plow the snowfields with that thing."

Clay took Todd's hand in his own, rubbing a fingertip between the creases in her knuckles. "No, you're the hardy type, I can tell," he said gently. "Not a laborer, but. Tough. Scarred. You hide it behind that gorgeous face, but..."

He reacted with tender recognition, spreading his palm as Todd's hand balled into a fist under his touch. "There's no hiding this. You've got a fighter's pain."

Todd didn't answer. She swallowed hard, watching Clay's motions carefully, mentally testing the defenses of her own will. If she tried to guess how many years it had been since a man had examined her like this—had been allowed this close to her—she knew she'd come up short no matter her answer.

Clay redirected. "You said you've been away a long time; I took that to mean you consider this home. Where were you 'away' to, then, and what kept you there so long?"

Todd shook her head. "Away was... away. Not here." It would take too much out of her to try and explain the existence of the shadowed forests to an uninitiated civilian. Clay deserved better than to have his night ruined by the morbid details of her past life. She kept it simple.

"I had a family—a husband. He was a contractor, like you, worked a lot of remote infrastructure jobs near here, close to the mountains. Things didn't work out, he left. Took our savings, and our rover, left me the cabin."

"Holy shit." Clay's eyes went wide. "Did they ever find him? The authorities, I mean?"

"Nah. Fucker got away clean. Never did find him. After that, I didn't know what to do with myself now that I was all alone again after so many years. Got fed up with myself; who I had become. So, I took a long trip through the mountains. Reconnected with nature."

"Completely understand," Clay nodded. "Done exactly that myself."

Todd gave a wry smile. "Maybe not exactly."

"And as for why you came back?"

Todd traced a fingertip around the mouth of her bottle. "Ever heard stories about those people who wake up in the middle of the night and don't know why, then come to find out the next day someone they loved just died?"

Clay gave a half-shrug.

"I had a bad night like that. Had this sickness, in my stomach—couldn't shake it. Kept getting this warning in the back of my head like I should check on my people. Made the trip up to my mom's old lakehouse, up in the caldera. There were appraisers there getting ready to auction off her belongings to the locals."

Clay set his bottle down. "Man, I'm sorry. That's rough. How did she go?"

"Probably the same way she always went about her business. No doubt she was cussing out the spirits that took her all the way down."

Clay suppressed a laugh. "Sorry. Don't mean to disrespect."

Todd waved it off. "It's fine. We weren't close—or, maybe we were, but we never liked each other much. I gave up trying to live up to the standards of someone who had none at a young age. She didn't miss me when I was gone any more than I miss her now. Maybe that was just how she liked it."

A silence settled between them. There was a bowl of peppernuts on the bar; Todd began rolling one between her fingers, hesitating before she continued.

"Can I ask you a question?"

Clay met Todd's gaze, a wry smile tickling the stubbled corners of his mouth. "Shoot."

Todd swallowed again. "What's the thing you're most afraid of in life?"

"Not all skin-deep after all, then." Clay smirked, exhaling thoughtfully. "I'd have to say... being forgotten by the people I love most. In this life or the next, just. That kinda thing scares the shit outta me."

"Being forgotten..." Todd furrowed her brow, visibly pained. "... Or forgetting?"

Clay just smiled that wry smile. "What a question, coming from the girl who can't remember her own name."

*

"You see, I listened in on that little deal you were offered by the treefolk," Cornell was saying loudly, ignoring the pained screams of the man beneath him. "Considering I've a wee bit more pull than you in matters regarding this realm we inhabit, I've a deal of my own to offer, one that mayhaps could earn ye some lenience from those pesky mimics."

Travers held his hands in front of his face, as if holding something back, but his efforts were in vain—his skull was reshaping itself, growing outwards, pushing his fingers out and away like the breaking of a levee.

Grinding teeth and bone popping like drywood accompanied the growth of a bestial snout, a trickle of blood seeping from his widening nostrils as they took on a wide and boxy shape. His hands went to the top of his head instead, attempting yet again to suppress another growth beneath his lined cap. His mistake. Dark, branchlike growths sprouted from within his skull in a burst of viscera that splashed across Todd's feet, prompting her to take a step back from the transforming man. Travers renewed his pained screams with a rising fervor, as the branches Todd now saw were actually antlers had pierced the hunter's hands, splitting them apart as if he'd tried to pull apart razor wire. With no choice afforded to him, Travers pulled both arms down, hard. His hands slipped off the ends of his wrists like the tattered remains of a pair of gloves—and in their place, capping the ends of his unusually slender arms, were the unmistakable black sheen of a set of cloven hooves.

"He's quite the dramatic sort, aye?" Cornell tittered, paying almost no heed to Travers as the changing man fell to all fours, continuing to grow outwards from himself in all sorts of violent new ways. "As I was sayin'. I know your type, lass. I know the look—ye thought the world below would accept you in this self-declared state of emergency, evacuated from the mortal world ye were born inta. Nae, Missy, nae—we like the quiet down here, in the shadows. Ye nae gettin' a free pass to come and go as ye please, like we're one of those fancy human resorts with their strange vittles and servantfolk. You'll nae get to run away from

Eat

yourself just by intruding in our homes, no
matter how long ye spend hiding behind that
scary face. You're no proper beastie—not like
our friend here is becoming."

Travers craned his bulging neck back,
the skin of his throat and face seeming to split
along an invisible seam—dark purple burst
forth, what appeared to be coils of muscle and
soft tissue at first revealing to be a glistening wet
hide. All at once, the taut, straining membrane
of man flesh burst apart, and from within a fully
grown elk spilled out into the snow, steam rising
from his velvet that still had scraps of his former
self clinging to it like afterbirth.

"He... hel... p... m... mee... "

The final words spoken in human
tongue by the former Travers gave way to a low,

abrasive groaning, his new vocal cords scraping against his much broader throat. Uneducated in the art of walking upright on all four limbs, the uncoordinated bull elk kicked helplessly up at the air from his position in the snow, laying on his side and tossing his head pitifully.

"Ych â fi! 'Tis the miracle of life. What a handsome critter he makes, aye?" Cornell wobbled happily on his branch, fluttering his wings to readjust them. "Ahem. Now, with that nastiness out of the way, we can begin our game! It's called: 'Take It, Or Feck Off', and it's absolutely bangin', trustsee. Goes a l'il summat like this: I offer ye a deal, and either ye take it— or, ready for this?—ye feck off!"

Todd felt her hands trembling in disgusted rage. She reached up, wiping her chin dry with the backside of her wrist. "Spit it out already. You're wasting everyone's time with this psycho bullshit."

Cornell recoiled somewhat. "Taw. Ye got smoke pourin' out them ears, gally. Och. Hate to be the magpie yankin' your tail. Hate to be a magpie at all, really, feckin' blighters." He gave a performative clearing of his throat, drawing his diminutive self up to his full height. "Now! The deal is quite generous, if'n I do say so meself, in that I've tailored it to your needs. In fact, in takin' this deal, I'll even be willing to overlook the offense you laid at me feet earlier, and let your riddle go unanswered! All ye have to do is this."

The raven alit from his perch, wings flapping to slow his fall before he caught himself once more upon the transformed elk's antlers, hanging off them as if they were just another branch. "Be yourself. Be a good beastie to match this beastie here, let the bear out. And have yourself some supper."

Todd was aghast. "You're disgusting."

"Ew ia? Nae, I'm simply offerin' ta help ye be who you've been tryin' so hard to be since you came to our humble little forest." Cornell gyrated in place slightly, keeping his balance as the weakened Travers was losing energy fast, unable to do much but raise his head for a moment and bleat wearily. "Take a few bites, dig in! Give the animal in ye summat to nosh on. Once I've seen ye eat enough of poor old Travers here to convince me, I'll let the tree-kin know you're the genuine article, and we'll make another deal. One that lets Mama Bear stay at home in these woods for good."

Eat

*

It seemed only moments later they were back at the inn and Todd had climbed atop him, Clay's bed as warm and welcoming to her as any had ever been. Her vision swam once her legs had wrapped around his hips, Clay piercing her outermost defenses with his eyes always on target, smiling up at her all the while. There was work to be done, and though Todd was no laborer, Clay definitely was. Piece by piece he broke her down, softening every part of herself she laid bare for him. Todd fed herself to this stranger, and Clay had his fill, lips moving in agonizing tandem with hips. When Todd took his face in her hands, seizing control, Clay wrested it back from her with another one of his clever smiles and a firm grip on whatever part of her she'd left unattended. She was utterly defenseless before this man; more importantly, she knew she was completely safe.

Until she slid her arm around his back, her fingers slipping between the grooves in Clay's spine, and in a moment of stark realization she found it was a perfect fit.

Like she'd been burned suddenly, Todd leapt back, dismounting in a panic.

"Whoa whoa, easy girl," Clay breathed, reaching out in confusion. He wiped a bead of sweat from his brow, keeping a respectful distance even as he offered comfort. "Something wrong? I thought we—you were incredible, did I hurt something, or..."

Todd pulled the covers up, shaking her head. She squeezed her eyes shut, trying to banish the sensory memory of another night, much like this. Too much like this. "No, it's not you," she said, not knowing herself if it was a lie. "I'm sorry, you've been great. I'm not... I wasn't ready for this. Not yet. I thought I was. I thought wrong."

Clay gulped in lungfuls of air, trying to regain his bearings as well as his breath. "Okay. Okay, sure, fine. Yeah, no problem. I get it. You don't gotta explain. Uh, hang on." His arms went out to his sides, Clay searching for something with rapid jerks of his head—he located the underwear Todd had discarded at the foot of the bed, folded into the displaced sheets, and quickly offered them up to her. "Here. G'head, get yourself back some privacy, and when you're ready we can talk about it."

With wet eyes and a grimace, Todd stared back at Clay, and he quickly course-corrected. "Or, not talk about it? Whatever you wanna do, it's fine. Take your time, keep it to yourself—I'll let this go at your pace. Really, it's fine."

Todd hid her face in a hand, turning away from Clay to conceal a tear. "Fuck. I'm sorry. I let it go so far, I don't know, I thought... maybe if I just don't make a big deal of it, just act like this is business as usual... if there was nothing to regret, then there wouldn't be any consequences. Stupid."

"No, it's not stupid at all," Clay assured her, quickly pulling his pants on. "I understand, really. I'm just, I'm happy I got to let you give it a try—listen," he said, pushing his sweaty bangs out of his eyes. "I've been there. I mean, not exactly where you've been, obviously. But I've left an open wound unattended. We all think we're so tough, right, that we can just grit our teeth and push through?"

Todd gave a shaky sigh, and Clay sat up against the headboard, bringing his legs to his chest above the covers. "You've been great tonight. This has been... you've been the most fun I've had in... I don't even know how long. I thought this whole trip would have been a bust, right up 'til I walked into that sleepy little pub and saw you." He chuckled, then stopped himself. "Last thing I wanna do is put my nose where it don't belong, or give you the wrong impression. I'm not foolin' myself with any kind of expectations. You come and go as you please, this is just a room to me. I'm a guest in your little town."

"My town." Todd winced. "At this point I'm as much a stranger here as you.

Everyone I knew is long gone. I don't recognize it anymore." She paused. "Or myself."

Clay was still somewhat lost, but dutifully tried to follow along. "So, what's... stopping you from moving on? Moving away, I mean?"

"I guess I feel like..." Todd sniffed, folding her arms together over herself. "Maybe I don't deserve to."

"Ah, bullshit." Clay chuckled. "Let me ask you somethin', might be a... weird question. D'you pray at all?"

Todd shook her head.

"I don't mean like, y'know," Clay stammered, waving his hand about overhead. "Not necessarily the big important conversations with a religious entity. D'you ever just... commune with yourself, alone, in the quiet? Y'know. Meditate? Reflect?"

Todd nodded. "Too much, sometimes."

Clay bit his lip, scratching at the stubble of his chin. "Yeah, see. I won't tell you that's a bad thing, 'cos it ain't. But I will tell you what my old man used to tell me, when I'd get the blues and couldn't seem to lift the world off myself."

"What's that?"

Clay turned, giving another soft smile. "Sometimes to see a new day, you gotta burn the old one down."

Todd pondered this. She reached out her own hand to take Clay's.

"I had a good night, Clay. I hope I didn't ruin your trip."

He gave a dismissive wave. "You're the only thing about this trip I'm gonna remember. Maybe someday I'll come back through here and wander on into your sleepy little pub again."

Todd nodded. "Maybe I'll be there when you do."

Immolate

Todd stared down at Travers, his eye staring up at her, wide and frantic. "Is this about me," she asked coolly, "Or about him? I'm not so sure."

"Isn't everything about you?" Cornell asked sternly, momentarily forgetting his playful tone of voice. "Isn't that why you're here, in this place? Looking out for yourself? Nursing those old wounds?"

Todd shook her head. "Nah. I get it. You want me to think I have something to learn from you. Like you actually have some lesson to teach with your games, your riddles."

She turned and bent down, reaching for the pack. Cornell watched curiously, somewhat taken aback. "Oh, you know what's in this mind, do ye? Got me scam all figgered out, yeh?"

"Yes." Todd turned back with Downsey's rifle in one hand, pointing it directly at the elk's head and blasting the poor creature into the next life. The gunshot sent Cornell flying off his perch and back up into the trees above.

"Godammit gally, the feck was that about?!"

Todd tossed the spent rifle away carelessly. "He was dead no matter what. I saw no value in letting you keep dragging it out any longer."

Cornell was fuming as he hopped closer on his chosen branch, the puffed-up raven clacking his beak in agitation. "That's twice now, ye feckin' cunt. Twice you've denied me satisfaction."

"I've a reputation for that," Todd said dryly.

The tengu spirit seethed, the air around him seeming to ripple in radiating waves of heat. "Aye, mun, aye. I see ye now. Alright. Alright, then. No deal. Fine. Not interested, I see. That's unfortunate, but aye, I understand. You're still on the hook for answerin' me riddle, and now ye went and put yourself in the worst place to be."

"And where's that?"

Cornell beat his wings, preparing to take flight once more. "On my last *fucking* nerve."

And with a frustrated caw into the morning dark, he was gone, disappearing into the treetops.

The gunshot had disturbed the kuaneach child—Todd kneeled beside the pack as it shifted about, reaching under the flap to offer a few soothing strokes. "Shh. Go back to sleep, it's over. Sorry about all that noise; that bird was being very naughty."

The way forward was clear, at the unfortunate expense of the late Travers. Todd looked down at the pitiful corpse and sniffed, wondering if she was losing her taste for this sort of thing. Ordinarily, she wouldn't have hesitated—eating one meal versus another, it should have made no difference. Elk meat was elk meat.

She reassured herself that it was Cornell. Todd simply didn't want to be dancing on anyone else's strings.

That was the best excuse she could give herself right now.

Todd shouldered the heavy pack, giving it another pat and cooing gently, coaxing the drowsy infant inside back to sleep. Up ahead, the mouth of the cave waited.

End of the line.

*

There were two cases of the stuff—the highest proof liquor the general store carried, courtesy of the late Joules. Todd wore a long coat, the pockets stuffed with matchbooks, a case under each arm. Standing on the porch of her old cabin, she saw little in it worth salvaging—time and the elements had leeched what beauty it once held, leaving behind only a desiccated shell. Grime and growth had sprouted from every crack and crevice, oozing sorrow until the logs were split and warped. Even the rotten porch threatened to collapse beneath her boots.

The perfect kindling for a bonfire.

She kicked open the weathered door, the cracked glass in their panes crumbling like shards of sugar. There was a dutiful bounce in her step as she stomped her way through the foyer, past the den and down the hall, coming to the kitchen—the centermost room of the house. Sweeping aside the withered remains of old papers and books, she let the whole mess clatter to the ground to make room for the cases, popping their wooden lids with her bare hands.

Immolate

In each case, a dozen bright green bottles, and one by one she uncorked each with hand and teeth alike. Once they had all been opened, the air filling with the suffocating vapors, Todd took two bottles between the four fingers of each hand. She knew the layout of the cabin intimately; best to start in the back of the house and move her way in a circle, leaving the route back down the hall towards the exit clear.

Judd's room was first. Wasting no time with collecting mementos or trinkets, blotting out any images that leapt to mind of seeing him getting ready for school in the morning, she overturned the bottles of one hand and let the contents drain all over his bed. When they were just about empty, she lobbed both bottles haphazardly into the open closet that still held his clothes, their remaining dregs bursting like little wet starbursts on the dusty floor. One hand produced a matchbook from a coat pocket, and Todd struck the whole wafer across the rough texture of the wooden door jamb. It flared brightly, already hungry, and she let the burning booklet fall to the soaked bed. It went up like a festive holiday, and without waiting to see the rest of the room be consumed, she turned heel and moved across the hall.

Jeanie's room. Separating the bottles into both hands, one dumped the liquor into the bassinet they hadn't thought to take out. She was old enough to have her own bed; a miniature little thing, looking more fit for a household pet than a human girl. Jeanie had never been given the chance to grow big, Timber's special treatment he administered her keeping her underdeveloped even into her fifth year. Her toys were still scattered across the plush blue rug in the center of the room. Todd tossed the second bottle straight up into the ceiling, the glass and liquid raining down in equal measure, making the whole room sparkle. A matchbook in each hand, Todd lit them both off one another and let them fall from her outstretched arms, twin serpents of flame racing up the painted flowers of her daughter's wallpaper.

Room by room, she went, restocking her supply of bottles as she crossed the house in a grid pattern, splashing every other wall as she went. The hallway bathroom. The pantry. The dining gallery. She threw bottles into corners with the deliberate patience of an old shaman throwing salt. She soaked the paintings hanging on the walls until their oil canvases peeled and dripped. Todd left no room undoused, no bottle unburst. Every floor and wall was a target, and Todd pitched the exploding bottles of hooch until her elbows creaked.

The last room untouched: their old bedroom. Hers, and Timber's.

Todd didn't even want to look inside. She stood at the doorway, scanning the vague shapes of the furniture in her peripheral vision. Even then, she almost felt a twinge of panic, like Timber's blurry silhouette might step forth from behind the window curtains. Four bottles—one underhanded toss sent two of them scattering their contents, a second toss the third bottle. The fourth she held in her hand, gazing into its sea-green reflections, even as she lit the final matchbook. Todd lifted the bottle, imagining it had just been handed to her by

Joules, or Yao. She took a steep swig, letting it burn her inside and out, just as she was doing to the cabin.

It scrubbed away what little regret she had left in her. She flicked away the matchbook, and the dark bedroom glowed bright orange behind her as she marched back down the hall.

The shadows were beginning to retreat, banished by the spreading flames that were filling each room now. With half a case left, Todd kicked the whole thing off the countertop, creating a small lake in the middle of the kitchen. Now, it was time to leave.

She'd almost forgotten how cold it was outside, pulling the coat about herself as she exited the front door once more, stepping lightly off the porch steps and crossing the gravel yard. There was a tree stump about a hundred yards away, clean and level, where she and Timber had split firewood once upon a time. Reaching it, Todd turned to face the cabin and took a seat. The show was just starting, and she had the best seat to watch it from.

Evening sunlight filtered from beyond distant treetops and between mountain bevels, but even the late day sky wasn't as bright as the dying star that had consumed Todd's former home. The flames had punched their way through the roof, layers of hard work and careful craftsmanship being burned away like papery flesh. In just under an hour, only the brittle skeleton of the blackened structure remained, yet the fiery nova at its center burned just as strong, as if fueled by Todd's sheer determination to see it welcome the coming nightfall.

She intended to burn this whole day down to welcome the next, after all.

Tomorrow, she'd return to the shadowlands. This time for good.

*

From outside, the cave appeared dark, though the further in Todd travelled, the brighter it became. Luminescent crystals. They sprouted from the walls like mushrooms, glowing soft indigo that spread outwards from their growths in gently flickering puddles. Even stepping between the clusters embedded in the cave floor cave the illusion of treading on the surface of water, the reflections in the crystals causing their glowing facets to shift and ripple as Todd passed them by. The cave sloped down at a smooth, even grade. No twists and turns, no traps or precarious terrain—Todd was simply hiking down steadily into the bowels of the mountain. Credit where credit was due, as the brightly illuminated cave made for an ideal place to set up base camp for any traveler.

The tunnel curved sharply, opening up into a wide space, the stone ceiling only a few feet above Todd's head—at its center, a stone column, surrounded by more crystals and other formations.

This was the place, no doubt, Todd's final destination. A small lean-to had been erected against the far wall of the cavern, a lantern hanging from one edge illuminating the piled rucksacks and sleeping rolls beneath it. Todd crossed the cavern quickly; she knew she was alone, there was no need for caution. The kuaneach infant in her backpack was only slightly larger than the average human child, which meant somewhere among these packs—

There. Behind the stacked sleeping rolls, two more packs just like the one Todd carried. Their design was unmistakable at this point: squared frames, solid bottoms, meant for retaining their shape to protect the fragile contents within. Just the sort of thing you'd stuff troublesome children into when they got bitey.

Todd kneeled beside the packs, setting down the one she carried alongside them. There was life in them, gently stirring.

All she needed was proof of life, and she'd be on her way. Todd reached for the other two packs—

A thunderclap deafened Todd. She stumbled on her knee, her weight shifting suddenly. Weird. Todd was confused, momentarily losing her balance. She reached up to feel at her shoulder—why was it wet?

The gunshot didn't register as such until well after she'd snapped back to her senses and dove behind the stone column, narrowly avoiding the second shot that embedded itself in the wooden frame of the lean-to. She'd gotten sloppy. Overconfident. The only hunter she'd successfully outsmarted tonight, and she left him alive to catch up to her. Stupid. Todd squeezed her gushing shoulder tight, unable to suppress her panting groans—the large caliber bullet had glanced off her shoulder blade, but that didn't make the wound any less devastating, her arm gouged open down to the bone.

And right on cue, the lecture began.

"Shoulda killed me, bitch!" Downsey shouted triumphantly. "Not so smart now, are ya? Nowhere to hide, no more tricks left to pull! I told the other three—see, *they* were the real science-types, *they* were the ones afraid to pull a trigger. Look where that got them! And look where you are now, stuck in here with me, the triggerman! I got you..."

He was growing louder, stomping closer—

"Right... in... my—"

Impatient as ever—

"—*Sights*!"

Downsey's next overeager shot blasted a few inches off the tops of a couple stalagmites, but Todd had already rolled out of harm's way, anticipating his movements.

"I'll admit, you had me going for a while," he continued, racking another round as the spent brass clattered to the cavern floor. "The job was to retrieve some kids—shapechangers. Natural-born, unprecedented! They warned us it was a whole family of wolves; they didn't say anything about a bear-shifter in these parts. Should've known it was you with that stupid little berrypicker ruse you pulled on me. No matter—"

Todd only narrowly dodged the next shot, Downsey standing exactly where she had been only a few moments ago, placing himself between her and the children. Another yank of the bolt, and the casing pealed brightly as it bounced off the stone ground. In her current form, a direct hit from that rifle would tear her in half. She needed to shift, fast. Gritting her teeth, Todd began to focus...

"I know what comes next," Downsey continued to bluster, interrupting Todd's thoughts. "The bear comes out, rips me limb from limb, yeah? Well, before you decide to rush me, consider this: the safety of these young'uns you're so keen to protect."

Todd cautioned a peek around the column—sure enough, Downsey had his rifle lowered, aimed directly at the packs on the ground. All three were gently stirring, the sedating infants frightened by the gunshots and shouting.

"You hurt them, you're burned," Todd argued, attempting to call his bluff. "No money in the corpses of children. You kill them, you don't get paid, dickhead. Your friends would have all died for nothing."

"I'm burned, am I?" Downsey grinned evilly, the glint of a false tooth catching the light of the cavern. "What did I just say, girl? I'm the triggerman. You see, those other three, the science heads... if it were any of them in here with you, you'd be absolutely right. Payment on delivery. Except I'm special. It's my job to protect those other poor bastards. Now, I'll be the first to admit it... I didn't exactly meet expectations on that front this time around. But that doesn't change the fact that my contract was negotiated separately from theirs', and I have a few terms that are non-negotiable. Certain conditions gotta be met before I ever sign on that dotted line. The most important of them being..."

Downsey reached out with his rifle, using the barrel to unhook the lantern hanging off the lean-to. The flame flickered haphazardly within, the kerosene splashing about as the lantern dangled off the tip of his weapon.

"I always get paid in advance."

Todd's stomach sank as Downsey flicked his wrist upward dramatically, dislodging the metal handle from the end of his rifle.

And the lantern fell.

Hunted

Though the lanterns on the walls were all dimmed, the sunlight shining in from behind did well enough to illuminate the ordinarily dark pub. It was still morning, leaving no mystery as to why the pub was empty. Some part of Todd had hoped Clay would be waiting there for her to say goodbye before he set off. A gut feeling she'd had, like maybe this was a thread not worth severing just yet. Maybe there was some value yet to be had in clinging to it, that it may yet prove a lifeline to lead her back to shore.

"Hey! Hey, Todd!"

Maybe her gut instinct wasn't so far off after all.

Todd turned to see Clay through the wide archway separating the pub from the rest of the inn, travel bags in both hands and strapped to his back as he trudged down the stairs. He was smiling wide at her, apparently as happy and surprised to see her as she was him.

"Come back for another round?" Todd joked, her boots echoing about the empty pub as she climbed the short steps back up into the inn's space, resting her weight against the stair's railing. "Little early for knocking back."

Clay scoffed affectionately. "Big words coming from you. You looked about ready to hop over that bar in there and start wheezing on the tap."

Todd laughed, once more feeling embarrassed by the sound. Like Clay was teasing out of her the part of herself she'd tried to bury beneath her stoicism and quiet nature. She still couldn't decide if she enjoyed it.

Maybe the fact that she'd come back to see him off should have helped provide the answer.

"You got any idea if you'll be in the area again anytime soon?"

Clay shook his head. "Nah, sorry. I go where the work takes me. Of course, if the opportunity arose; a job crops up somewhere near here, I'd take it in a heartbeat. These mountains, though? This topography is... well. Expansive. Even if I get a contract 'near' here, I could still be miles and miles away, separated by a couple of mountains."

Todd smirked. "Well, the average grizzly bear can travel up to fifty miles in a single day. Give me a ring when you're close, I'm sure I can at least make that distance."

Clay laughed, completely missing Todd's joke. "You're a real peach, Todd. I'm happy I got to meet you."

Feeling somewhat crestfallen, Todd concealed it with a warm smile, patting the railing as she saluted. "Happy I met you too, Clay. I'll hold out hope for a bridge to collapse up the road somewhere."

As she turned to leave, she heard scuffling behind her, like Clay was trying to make up his mind about which direction to go.

"Uh, hey, wait a sec, Todd, wait!"

He trundled up to her after dismounting the stairs, leaving his bags behind to catch up. Todd felt a little thrill in her chest.

"Listen." Clay leaned in close, looking around as if making sure no one was eavesdropping. "Marshawn Falls. You know it?"

"Of course."

Clay shifted nervously. "I shouldn't be telling you this, not because I don't trust you or anything, it's just..." He cleared his throat, dispelling his hesitation. "You said you had a husband, a contractor? Worked the area?"

Todd's breath caught in her chest.

"On my way up here, there was a... well, a nice way of saying it would be a 'miscommunication' of sorts, between dispatch and the locals. Someone else had already committed to the job before I got here, but the local office never contacted my people before they sent me out, so they had to eat the work order. Really pissed 'em off something fierce. Anyway, I was on the horn with dispatch, and at some point in the commotion, in the noise I heard some mention of who was on-site. They said he was an older guy, knew the area well, was trying to move back in on his old stomping grounds. He'd driven out all the way from Marshawn Falls, had packed up his whole kit and then some and taken the 'rover' over a few bridges to get there. I doubt it was him, older guy and all, but I figured it wasn't impossible you'd married someone outside your own age..."

"No." Todd nodded curtly. "Thanks for telling me. Probably someone else, you're right. Be seeing you, Clay."

He gave another humble nod, and returned to his bags. Todd felt her pulse rising, vision going tunneled as she exited the inn.

A detour had just been added to her itinerary for the day. On her way back to the Shadowlands, she'd be paying a visit to the falls.

*

Downsey had correctly predicted Todd's next move—setting the fire, he knew she'd make a run straight for the packs to get the children out of the way of the quickly spreading flames. Rifle already raised, a flash of dark fur leapt up into view, and he fired, blowing a hole straight through his mark.

There was no doubting Downsey's aim. His mistake was assuming Todd would have shifted into bear form at all. A few animal pelts fell into a heap, gunsmoke rising from the singed bullet hole that had passed clean through them.

Todd had skirted around the other side of the column, tackling Downsey and wrenching the rifle out of his hands before he had a chance to rack the next round. The two of them fell together—straight into the pool of flames. Todd landed on top, jamming the rifle butt into Downsey's chin, his cap and jacket quickly igniting. The leather clothes she wore were naturally fire retardant, unlike the hunter's plush all-weather apparel. A few seconds of enduring the heat against her bare arms and the screams rising from beneath her, then Todd rolled off Downsey, letting the man writhe in the fire as she grabbed at the three packs. It took all her strength to pull them to safety, well out of the radius of anything flammable, the stone chamber quickly filling with dark smoke.

The wound in her shoulder was still bleeding freely—Todd clamped her already red-soaked hand over it, watching Downsey's torment play out before her. The hunter had taken far too long to drag himself out of the flames, lacking the presence of mind to pull the burning clothes off of himself until well after his skin was scorched and the cave reeked of burning hair. The disintegrating jacket finally discarded, the portly man rolled around pitifully on the cold stone floor, patting away the last embers that still clung to his smoking thermal layers. When he was finally fully extinguished, Downsey collapsed against a stalagmite, curling into a fetal position and whimpering pitifully. The dark red skin of his cheek was sizzling, blisters already bubbling beneath the flesh all along the side of his neck and head.

"Help," he pleaded weakly. His voice was raspy, words coming between fits of coughing as a result of inhaling smoke. "Help, please. Please, I'm sorry."

The lean-to was burning to the ground, wooden struts cracking and spitting up bouts of burning ash. It wouldn't be long before this whole chamber would suffocate anyone left inside. And Downsey was in no condition to walk himself out now.

Todd picked up the dropped rifle, kneeling beside the trembling hunter, raising the weapon before him demonstratively.

"One," she said, racking the holt—an unspent rifle round was jettisoned from the ejection port.

"Two." A second pull, a second round pinged off the stone floor.

"Three." The third bullet landed square in Downsey's lap.

He looked at Todd fearfully, shrinking away somewhat, not understanding the point she was making. She threw the rifle away, straight into the burning heap of wood, before turning her angry eyes back upon him.

"Three children you stole, you and your friends. Taken from their mothers. On its own, one would be a death sentence—where do you think that leaves you now?"

Downsey didn't answer, clutching pitifully at his burned cheek.

"The kuaneach," Todd continued. "Where did he come from? He doesn't have a family in these woods, I would know about it. Who did you steal him from, and why?"

Downsey shook his head. "Found... we found him..."

Todd slapped Downsey across the face, hard enough to make a blister pop. He wailed out, shuddering in agony as his overstimulated nervous system began to shut down.

"Please, it's the truth," he babbled. "In the woods, in the snow—a hollowed out tree... left there, alone, we don't know... where he came from..."

"Admitting freely to abducting a child without even knowing or caring where they came from isn't the winning defense strategy you think it is," Todd remarked dryly, wiping her hand on her knee. "Shapechanger children, I can understand. What could you possibly learn from using a kuaneach as a research specimen?"

Downsey shook his head. "Different. Somehow... he's... unusual..."

"Forget it, I don't care." Todd looked the wounded man up and down one final time. He was clearly suffering, in more pain than she could ever hope to inflict on him at this point. Without being rushed to a practiced surgeon soon, he would surely be dead within a day or two. The merciful thing would be to rip his throat out—end it quickly.

She'd been here before, she realized. Facing this same choice, in circumstances altogether not too dissimilar from these.

Todd's fingers tightened, thickening, her hand shifting into a heavy paw as the wicked sharp bear claws began to scrape across Downsey's face.

"What's the thing you're most afraid of in life?"

*

The current was strong enough coming off the falls that Timber had an easy time washing his clothes in the river, the older man fishing his freshly rinsed shirt out of the foaming waters before wringing it dry. The rover was parked nearby, at the water's edge; Timber hung the dripping shirt on the clothesline he'd strung up between the vehicle and a nearby tree. The simple task was slow-going, requiring him to exert himself somewhat, his back and knees not as flexible as they once were. Hair thin and gray, parts of him sagging that were once firm—age had caught up with him, to say nothing of the watcher in the trees close by.

His chores done for the day, Timber made for the rover, hefting himself up the steps laboriously and through the screen door. There was a minifridge directly inside, and Timber wasted no time in procuring himself a cold brew from within its inner door. Every flat surface of the cramped living space was covered in empty liquor bottles or cans of ale; Timber had to sweep a couple cans off his favorite chair before settling in, cracking open the can and beginning

Hunted

the long process of numbing himself into his
evening torpor.

Mothers

"Mama?"

"Yes, dear."

"Play hide and seek with us."

It wasn't a request. Judd put forth his demand with absolute authority, and Todd had no choice to obey. Setting aside the dish she was drying, Todd wiped her hands on a cloth and turned to glare down at her progeny.

"And if I refuse?"

Judd stared back defiantly. "I'll eat *all* the pie in the icebox."

"Oh yeah?" Todd advanced on him, arms crossed; behind her older brother, Jeanie was giggling, burying her face in his back. "You're gonna eat that whole thing? Go ahead, you'll explode like a balloon; then I'll never need to make any more pies ever again!"

"Nawww!" Judd laughed, a wheezing, labored sound—the oxygen concentrator he wore only really seemed noticeable when he laughed like that, the tubing in his nostrils whistling and the little box-shaped machine bouncing against his hip. "I'm gonna eat it all, and then I'll be as big and fat as *you*!"

"That's it! You're on, dummy." Todd leaned down, curling her fingers into scary claws as she pretended to hunt the two children, sending them scampering down the hall. "I'm gonna get you both and eat you all up. Better hide good this time, I mean it...!"

But they were already gone, having found their favorite hiding spaces. Todd returned to finish drying the dish, beginning counting loud enough for them to hear her from down the hall. "One, two, three, four..."

The counting trailed off. Todd quieted herself to listen closely. She couldn't hear the stomping of little feet. The children had gone eerily quiet.

"Judd?"

Todd set down the dish, wiping her hands on a tablecloth. She waited for a response. Slowly, she made her way out of the kitchen, down the hall.

"Jeanie?"

The hallway was dark, the shadows of the advancing day hanging from the ceiling like black cobwebs. Todd crept towards the children's bedroom, listening carefully. No giggles or hushed whispers could she detect. No humors or pranks awaited her. The closer she drew to that door, the more she felt dread rising from the pit of her restrained self. The terrors that existed only in a mother's worst nightmares, manifesting first as a passing thought, then growing with each measured step she took. Until she stood before the door, a hand outstretched. It began to shake.

The game was over, she knew, even before she opened that door.

"Kids? Mommy's coming."

She didn't say it so much as promise it. There was a single, tiny sob from within.

Todd turned the knob.

*

Clutching a beaded shawl about herself, Wolfmother emerged from her dark den into the morning, eyes red and puffy from a night spent crying. She was in disbelief, sinking to her knees, both hands reaching out to open both of the backpacks that had been deposited on her doorstep. Son and daughter, both sound asleep, the cubs curled up in their warm little travel bundles.

Pulling them both close, fresh tears burst forth, Wolfmother cradling her pups together against her chest in both arms—she looked out, towards the horizon, searching for her savior. Just beyond the treeline, she saw her: the weathered old grizzly, watching from a detached distance, a third pack still strapped to her back. Wolfmother knew Todd needed no words of thanks, and gave only the slightest of nods in appreciation.

The gesture was received without fanfare—Todd turned away, limping away into the dense trees beyond, returning the same way she'd come. Though she had returned Wolfmother's cubs, there was still work to be done elsewhere. Another child to be returned home safely.

There was always work to be done. Wolfmother could sleep soundly now, reunited with her family—but Todd had a long way to go before she could rest.

Come nightfall, the spirits would emerge from the trees once more. They would be looking for her. She had overstayed her welcome, and was grateful to be allowed this final reprieve before her departure from the Shadlowands.

And there was another newcomer in these woods.

She'd taken up the scent en route to Wolfmother's den. A scent somehow familiar in its strangeness: though she didn't know who it was, she knew the cloth this stranger was cut from. She herself wore it well. Pain and sadness; bloodied body and seeping wounds. It smelled half-rotten. Half-dead. She followed the trail now, back the way she came, albeit closer to the river.

Eyes on her. Todd felt her hackles rising even before she saw him. A ghostly apparition, rising from a half crouch in a distant snowbank, his profile framed against the darkness of the skeletal trees.

Todd had known shapechangers her whole life. She'd known men who became wolves, and wolves who remained wolves their whole lives. This one was different, in ways she couldn't hope to ascertain upon this single encounter. If it weren't for her keen sense of smell, she might have thought he was hewn from red clay. She knew the rusty red-brown soaking through his hide was blood, layers upon layers, caked with the mud and detritus of his travels. The beastman propped himself up weakly on a broken spear, one of relatively sophisticated design contrasting his savage appearance. Even at this distance, Todd could see the fiery amber glow of his eyes, darkly troubled, an unreachable soul trapped behind them.

Yet despite this, Todd felt an immediate kinship with this strange Wolf. Tatters of clothing clung to his shoulders; filthy remnants of a former life. His gnarled snout, scarred and permanently scowling, reminded her of the same expression she had worn on patrol through the woods. A mask to repel the meek and those who might seek to challenge her, protecting her inner sorrows. This was no feral lycan, nor was he a druid like Wolfmother: his truth lay somewhere in the middle, an altogether singular existence. He had more in common with Todd than any fey or common beast. A broken and battered traveler, looking for solace in isolation, to nurse his wounds and bury his troubles in the snow.

Todd huffed, shaking her shoulders to loosen the snow that had settled between them. She nodded at the stranger, giving silent acknowledgement.

The Wolf's grasp on his spear loosened somewhat, and he gave the slightest of nods in return.

Passing ships in the night.

The two warriors broke away from each other, resuming on their respective journeys. Todd, carrying the bundled infant to the forest's exit; The Wolf, into the forest's deepest reaches.

The following night would come peacefully, absent anymore intruders.

Absent the newly retired guardian of the forest. For a new guardian had arrived to take her place.

Between this stranger and Wolfmother, this forest belonged to the wolves now. It would be decades before another bear would call this place home.

Answer

The sun had yet to show its face from behind the clouds, despite the snowstorm having subsided some time ago. The light of the new day was kept at bay behind the cover of overcast gray—yet Todd trekked effortlessly through the snow, making for the outskirts of the forest once more, unbothered by the many hazards she'd faced on this same route several hours prior. She'd made it most of the way on all fours, but when she realized she was only a few minutes from leaving the Shadowlands for good, Todd was compelled to shift back to human form and complete the last leg of the journey accordingly. It may not have been the most efficient means of travelled, but it seemed the most fitting. Perhaps she'd make for the nearby town she'd lied to Downsey about having hailed from, play the part of a lost traveler searching for a ride back home.

The way she saw it, Todd had spent enough time as a beast to last her a lifetime. She was looking forward to another fresh start as herself.

"Toodle-feckin'-oo, gally. Glad to see ye farin' well after all that excitement, if'n a wee bit worse for wear!"

The victorious mood was soured in an instant, Todd wincing as she was brought to a halt by the familiar voice hailing her. "Is there really no one in the world your time is better spent harassing?" She bemoaned, turning to look up at the piebald raven above.

"None I enjoy feckin' with as much as ye, nope!" Cornell hopped forward happily, practically hanging sideways off the branch. He seemed positively delighted to see Todd again, which she knew did not bode well for her.

"I'll warn you now, I've had a long night and nothing to eat—I'll gladly take some roasted raven for a late lunch."

"Eugh!" Cornell was taken aback. "I offered ye dinner! Talk about ungrateful..."

The edge of the forest was close. So close, Todd could smell the faint wisps of civilization, pollution, and people. For once in her life, she dearly wanted to be among it all again.

"You know what I'm going to say, bird. Make it quick."

Cornell hopped forward again, peering suspiciously over Todd's shoulder. "I don't recall. Did we settle on terms for the ikkle tyke's passage?"

Todd held her tongue.

"Ooh, naughty naughty, always so naughty." Cornell fluffed his wings, and from somewhere beyond the world of the seen, Todd could hear the screams of his night's victims echoing in the raven's aura. "Did ye think, truly, I den't know ye was transporting live cargo? 'Fraid ye've got egg on YORE face now, love."

Todd clenched up. There was a sense of victory slipping through her fingers now, so near to the end. A sense that, no matter how uncaring she may have been for her own safety the night past, this new day brought with it a sense of purpose. She couldn't let Cornell have this child.

No matter what it cost her in return.

"I give up." Todd held up her hands pleadingly. She wasn't used to submission, but she did her best, bowing her head and closing her eyes so as not to let any trace of defiance be seen in them. "You're right. I should have played your games. I was unkind. The infant is coming with me... if you'll allow it."

She swallowed, digging deep. "And I truly hope you'll allow it."

"What a waste of a pretty face," Cornell sneered. "I like ye more when ye put up a fight. It makes me feel so..."

He shuddered in delight, searching for the right word. "... Killy."

Todd felt the bear awakening. She clenched down harder. Not now. Not yet.

"I don't suppose ye got a good look at our new arrival, aye?"

Todd opened her eyes. She kept her tone even, non-threatening. "I did. The beastman from afar."

"Far afar," Cornell agreed, making a sniffing noise. "Smelled like he had a proper trek gettin' here. Lots of blood on his conscience. Will be a right hoot, feckin' wit' em. Figger I aughta let you off the hook so he can take yer place, aye?"

Todd knew better. "But?"

"But!" Cornell cawed. "But but but. There's a wee debt needs resolving first. A payment owed in the form of a riddle solved. Resolve to solve, all debts are paid, aye aye, lass?"

Todd had lived a life of self-assuredness, not wasting time. She wasn't about to renege on that now.

"Let's hear that riddle again, then. I'm ready."

Cornell spun in place on his branch, already whistling a tune. He was drawing it out now, letting the tension build, keeping Todd in suspense. He froze as he saw the familiar look of annoyance begin to creep unbidden across her face, and winked approvingly.

"*What tears into flesh without tooth or claw.*

Invisible wounds that ceaselessly weep,

What icy season refuses to thaw,

The storm that denies the dreamer his sleep?

Take all you can carry, and walk with the dead,

And there'll be naught left of you to bury;

Keep none at all, less weight on your head,

And become the weight the living must carry."

The light of the day was growing brighter behind the gray veil of sky above. The birds were beginning to sing as if welcoming an early spring's arrival. And Todd, feeling the shifting weight of the kuaneach child strapped to her back, took a deep breath. There was only ever one answer she could think of—and, right or wrong, she knew in this moment everything would be alright from now on.

"I had a family once," Todd said, looking up at Cornell with a small smile. "Kids. Two of them. You would have liked them. They loved playing games like this. Hide and seek. Little puzzles. Making up riddles for me to solve. They were never very difficult—it was only ever about spending time with me. It was only make-believe, pretending I didn't know the answer every single time, just so I could make the games last longer. See them laugh one more time."

Cornell softened. The demon in him was momentarily quelled, and in its place, Todd recognized a childlike glee. "Sounds lovely, mum."

Todd exhaled. Mentally, she thanked her children. "The answer is memory."

The branch above her head clattered, snow sprinkling all around.

In a flash, the raven was gone, disappeared into another thread of time and space. The spirit was satisfied. Todd's sins were forgiven, and her passage was earned.

A single feather drifted down, mottled black and white. A parting gift. Todd reached a single hand up, palm spread, catching it in midair. It felt warm.

She pocketed the feather, tightening the straps on her shoulders one final time.

The world beyond was waiting.

Memento

"So how does it work, anyway?"

Todd traced a finger between the hairs on Timber's bare shoulder. "What do you mean?"

Timber shifted, propping his head up on his pillow, returning the favor of caressing Todd's naked arm. "The whole shapeshifting thing. Are you born with it? Do you get to choose the animal...?"

Todd nodded, tightening her lips somewhat. "Ah. You want the inside scoop, is that it?"

"Of course. About time we blew the lid off this thing. Years of global secularization ain't got nothing on the truth I'm about to bring to the world—the first human man to expose the druids and their dark magicks. Think of how famous I'll be."

"Yeah, I can see you hosting your own radioplay, for sure." Todd propped herself up to meet Timber's eyeline, considering which details were worth sharing. "So... no to the first question, yes to the second. At a young age we're expected to complete a ritual where we subsume our chosen animal."

Timber scoffed. "'Subsume'?"

"A polite way of saying kill. When we're old enough to hunt, we track down a member of our avatar animal's species, sacrifice it, and take on their form for the first time."

Timber furrowed his brow. "That's kinda... dark. I thought druids were all about nature and protection."

"Can't protect without knowing what it means to destroy. Besides, there's a lot of aspects and tenets to the faith I disagree with. It's why I wanted to get away—why I'm here with you, now."

"Okay, so," Timber sat up, puzzling the concept out loud. "The animal you kill literally becomes a part of you, is that it?"

"I guess it's a way of taking responsibility for your actions," Todd nodded. "Accepting that which you've killed into yourself, letting it become a part of you, each time you shift a living reminder of what you had to kill in order to become who you were meant to be."

"Is there any way to gain the ability to shape-change... you know, without the killing part?"

Todd pulled a face. "I've heard rumors. Druids who conceive and give birth in animal form. Supposedly their children are born with the ability, but I've yet to see it for myself. That kind of talk will also get you thrown out of certain circles—be careful not to bring it up again if ever you meet my mother."

"But not every druid has to go through with this ritual, right? It's not required?"

Todd stiffened somewhat. "Not strictly speaking, no. It's a personal choice."

Timber stared, but didn't press it. "So that means you killed a... a full-grown grizzly bear, then?" His eyes grew wide in realization. "By yourself? How, why...?"

Todd shrugged. "I don't know. Just to prove I could, maybe."

She looped her arm around Timber's back, sliding her slender fingers between the grooves of his spine. A perfect fit. "I think there's a part of me that is just... absolutist, in a way. I remember being so determined as a little girl to see the top of the mountain we lived on, I left home one morning and hiked all the way up. Took four days, got myself completely lost, ran out of food day one. Drank water out of leaves like I'd seen animals do in pictograph books. Eventually I got to the top, made it down into the caldera—where Niju found me, half-starved to death? That's where she built her lakehouse."

Timber chuckled. "Oh, so you've *always* been hardcore."

Todd considered this. "What's the thing you're most afraid of in life?"

"Being completely honest? Being mauled by a bear."

It took a moment, but Todd laughed at this, giving Tim a light shove. "Fine, be that way. Well, I never really knew what I was afraid of growing up. All the things the other kids in the village would say never made much sense to me. Spiders, the dark, being eaten alive. I grew up not knowing what to be afraid of, not knowing what could hurt me if I let it."

"Doesn't sound all that bad to me."

Todd leaned back against the headboard, breaking eye contact to look up at the ceiling.

"Then one night," she continued, "I had a dream. My first nightmare, really.

"I was walking through the village, a day like any other, going home after visiting my friend who lived down the main road a-ways. Not many big structures there; druids aren't really known for our architectural endeavors. So, when I get to my house, and I look up, and see it's been replaced by this giant building—so tall I could look straight up and never see the top of it. Tallest building I'd ever seen, like the skyscrapers in pictographs Niju had shown me from the outside world. And I'm thinking... where did this come from? Is this where I always lived? This would have taken ages to build; how long was I away for, how could I have missed it being built?

"So, I go inside. And at the ground floor, there's a desk, and someone asks for my name, and there's a line of people waiting to head up to their floor, going up the stairs. I get in line, wondering who all these people are, not recognizing any of them. I'm waiting for... hours, before the line starts moving, everyone taking the stairs one step at a time. Up and up, as slow as possible, everyone dragging their feet to get to their own floor. Each floor, someone steps off, and the line of people ahead of me is getting shorter, but the climb up only ever seems to get longer. The next floor, next person gets off, I'm starting to feel... strangely alone. I don't know any of these people, but when they get off, part of me misses them when they're gone. I'm starting to dread getting to the top floor, because once I'm there, I don't know who will be there with me. I start asking these people, these strangers, questions—who are you? Where did you come from, why are you here? No one has any answers; or at least, they don't feel like telling me. They all have their own business to attend to, and eventually, they're all gone. Stepped off onto their own floors. And I'm alone climbing these stairs.

"I'm near the top now. I take each flight after the next, and each floor is darker than the next, and I'm beginning to wish I hadn't come here at all. But I keep on. I keep climbing, reminding myself that this is my home. I'm meant to be here, more than anyone else, any of those strangers who left me to go about their own business down below. This is my home, not theirs. So, I climb, and keep climbing, until finally I'm at the top, standing at this door that looks like the door to my old room. The first bedroom I had, in the old cabin in the woods, before Niju moved us into the village. The room I was born in. I open the door, and I step inside, and it's so dark—dark enough that I'm beginning to see why the other kids I grew up with said they were afraid of the dark. But even still, I know I'm meant to be here, that I'm the only person that is meant to be here. I go in, and I look around, and there's... no one else. There's nothing waiting up for me at the top of that tower. The door shuts behind me; I'm in the dark, alone, crying out for someone. Anyone. Any of those strangers who left me on the climb up. They're not answering."

Timber was silent as Todd told her story, the troubled woman giving a great shuddering breath before she finished:

"They're not answering, and I know it's time to go to sleep. And for the first time, I'm afraid. Because at the top, in the dark, alone, waiting to fall asleep... I know the worst is still on its way."

*

There wasn't much left to salvage as far as the smaller items were concerned—wall portraits, utensils, other decorations, things of that nature—but most of the furniture had been left behind. When Todd arrived at Niju's lakehouse all those years ago, she'd interrupted the appraisers before everything could be auctioned off. In fact, had she followed instructions, Todd may have been able to recover the boxes of Niju's possessions that had already been carted off the premises before her arrival. She never bothered, though, having no real personal attachment to any of the items that had been taken. So, Todd sat now, in a kitchen without cookware or appliances, at a carved wooden table that had been too heavy to move, along with the matching chairs. Jeanie's high chair was still here as well, occupied now by a burbling little kuaneach child.

With her injured arm strapped across her front in a loose-fitted sling, Todd sipped at her mug of coffee, watching the infantile dragon snap playfully at the spoonful of mashed appleroot she was offering. The mug and silverware had both been reclaimed from Joules' old room above the shop, the metal cup bearing the old shopkeeper's name in etched lettering. It was all Todd was permitted to take with her. The new management wasn't so keen on kindling a personal relationship with this strange woman from the mountains who claimed to have been friends with the former shopkeeper... from almost a half century ago.

All things considered, Todd didn't have much reason to revisit Cherrystone after her latest trip into town. Nobody knew who she was anymore. The legendary bear had all but faded from the brochures as a novelty to excite the tourists with. Even Clay—

Todd didn't want to think about how many years it had been since her night with Clay. Since her final confrontation with Timber. Too many and not enough all at once. It was a disappeared opportunity, from a disappeared time, in a place that had all but itself disappeared from Todd's little world.

In the here and now, Indhea giggled, smacking her scaly little lips around the rim of the spoon wetly.

"Hey. You're making a mess," Todd scolded. She took another scoop from the bowl of appleroot, using the elbow of her injured arm to wipe Indhea's face clean. "You little dummy."

Indhea didn't seem to mind one bit. She was happy to make a mess, slurping down the final spoonful. And despite her protests, Todd realized she was happy to clean it up. With breakfast finished, Todd set aside the bowl. She presented Indhea with the little bear carving she always carried with her—it had become the infant's favorite toy, and Indhea happily accepted it, gumming idly at the wooden rump of the gifted token.

Todd would look for the child's parents soon enough. For today, she enjoyed having a little company.

The warm waters of the lake splashed languidly. Somewhere nearby, a flock of waterfowl cackled at one another, having returned from their migration and settling back into safer waters for the spring. The sun was just breaking the rim of the caldera, casting its amber light upon the scene.

Todd looked out at the lake through the wide window, watching the morning's arrival with a quiet appreciation. She wondered when the last time she'd enjoyed this view was.

Funny. Try as hard as she might, she couldn't remember.

Todd and Indhea's story will resume in

THE JACKAL ARDENT.